D0563329

ADLARD COLES MARITIME CLASSICS

MUTINY ON BOARD HMS BOUNTY

OTHER TITLES IN THE ADLARD COLES MARITIME CLASSICS SERIES

South (Ernest Shackleton) – ISBN 978-1-4729-0715-8
The Sea Wolf (Jack London) – ISBN 978-1-4729-0724-0
20,000 Leagues Under the Sea (Jules Verne) – 978-1-4729-0718-9

Forthcoming titles (published 2015)

Robinson Crusoe (Daniel Defoe) – ISBN 978-1-4729-1392-0
Lord Jim (Joseph Conrad) – ISBN 978-1-4729-1395-1

If you have any suggestions for titles you would like to see included in the series in future, please email us: adlardcoles@bloomsbury.com

MUTINY ON BOARD HMS BOUNTY

Comprising an account by Lieutenant William Bligh,
the vessel's master, with responses by Edward Christian,
lawyer, and brother of mutineer Fletcher Christian

Foreword by Pete Goss

ADLARD COLES NAUTICAL

BLOOMSBURY

LONDON • NEW DELHI • NEW YORK • SYDNEY

Published by Adlard Coles Nautical
an imprint of Bloomsbury Publishing Plc
50 Bedford Square, London WC1B 3DP
www.adlardcoles.com

Bloomsbury is a trademark of Bloomsbury Publishing Plc

First published 1790
First Adlard Coles edition published 2014

Foreword © Pete Goss 2014

ISBN 978-1-4729-0721-9
ePub 978-1-4729-0722-6
ePDF 978-1-4729-0723-3

Adlard Coles Maritime Classics (print) ISSN 2053-261X
Adlard Coles Maritime Classics (electronic) ISSN 2053-2628

A CIP catalogue record for this book is available from the British Library.

This book is produced using paper that is made from wood grown in managed,
sustainable forests. It is natural, renewable and recyclable. The logging and
manufacturing processes conform to the environmental regulations of the
country of origin.

Typeset in 10.75 pt, Haarlemmer MT by MPS Limited
Printed and bound in Great Britain by CPI Group (UK) Ltd,
Croydon CR0 4YY

Note: while all reasonable care has been taken in the publication of this book,
the publisher takes no responsibility for the use of the methods or products
described in the book.

CONTENTS

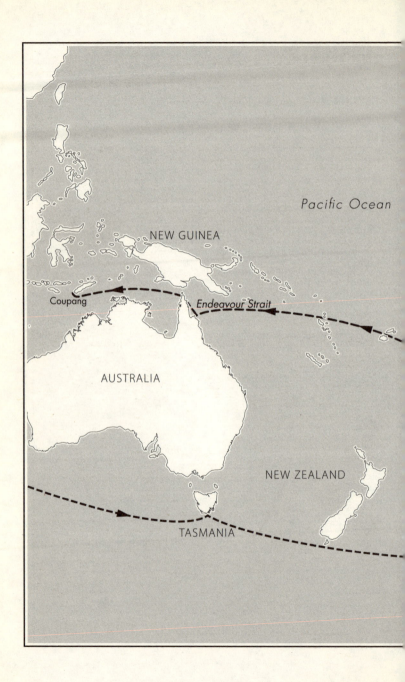

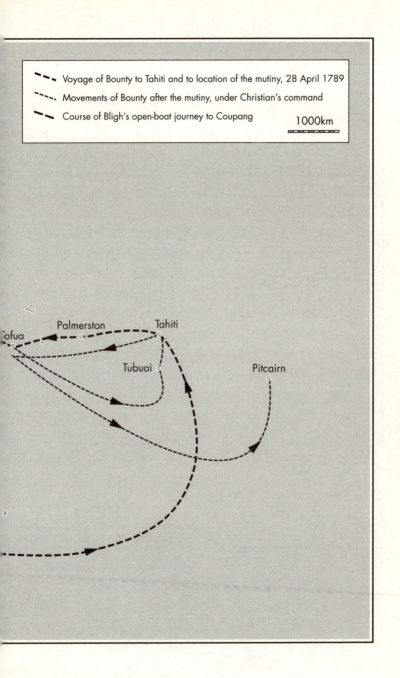

Voyage of Bounty to Tahiti and to location of the mutiny, 28 April 1789

Movements of Bounty after the mutiny, under Christian's command

Course of Bligh's open-boat journey to Coupang

1000km

Palmerston   Tahiti

ofua

Tubuai   Pitcairn

WILLIAM BLIGH

BORN 9 SEPTEMBER 1754, William Bligh joined the Royal Navy aged 7, serving as ship's boy aboard HMS *Monmouth* for two years between 1761 and 1763. He rose up through the ranks, and was chosen by Captain James Cook to be Sailing Master on HMS *Resolution* for Cook's third (and final) voyage to the Pacific in 1776.

During the American War of Independence, Bligh fought in several major sea battles, including the Battle of Dogger Bank (1781) and the Great Siege of Gibraltar (1782). Bligh left the Royal Navy following the end of the war and became a captain in the merchant navy. He returned to the Royal Navy in 1787 to command HMS *Bounty*.

After the mutiny Bligh continued his naval career and captained numerous vessels. He faced another mutiny in 1797, though this time as part of a widespread revolt by seamen that involved the crews of numerous ships.

During the Battle of Camperdown (1797), Bligh engaged three Dutch vessels, captured one and took a Vice-Admiral prisoner. He was also personally praised by Admiral Nelson for his actions during the Battle of Copenhagen (1801).

Bligh's authoritarian reputation secured him the role of Governor of New South Wales between 1806 and 1808, but he was later deposed in a rebellion.

He continued to advance in rank, becoming a Commodore, then Rear Admiral and ended his career as Vice Admiral of the Blue. He died in London on 7 December 1817.

EDWARD CHRISTIAN

Born on 3 March 1758, Edward Christian spent his childhood on the family estate in Cumberland (now Cumbria). His younger brother Fletcher was born when Edward was 6. Their father was descended from Isle of Man gentry, but after he died in 1768 their mother fell into severe debt and at one point faced the prospect of being sent to debtors' prison. Edward went to Cambridge, where he became friends with slavery abolitionist William Wilberforce, and later became both a judge and a professor of law.

CHRONOLOGY OF EVENTS

26th May 1787
The Royal Navy buys the collier *Bethia*, refitting her and renaming the ship HMS *Bounty*.

16th August 1787
32-year-old William Bligh is appointed the Commanding Lieutenant of the *Bounty*.

23rd December 1787
The *Bounty* leaves England, bound for Otaheite (now Tahiti), with the instruction to pick up a crop of breadfruit plants and transport them to the West Indies, where it is hoped they can be grown to provide a cheap food source for slaves.

25th April 1788
After a month of trying, in terrible weather conditions, Bligh abandons his attempt to round Cape Horn and plots a new course. He also demotes the *Bounty*'s Sailing Master, John Fryer, and replaces him with 24-year-old Fletcher Christian.

26th October 1788
The *Bounty* reaches Otaheite and spends five unplanned months there whilst Bligh waits for his breadfruit plant cargo to reach a sufficient level of maturity for transport. He allows the crew to live ashore and many become involved with local women.

Tensions rise, floggings become commonplace and several men try to desert.

4th April 1789
The *Bounty* leaves Otaheite with a cargo of over 1,000 breadfruit plants.

28th April 1789
Christian leads a mutiny against Bligh near Tofua, setting him adrift with 18 loyal crew in the ship's launch. Christian then returns in the *Bounty* to Otaheite, letting several Bligh loyalists leave the ship, and allowing locals to take their place aboard, including several women.

14th June 1789
Bligh reaches Coupang, Timor, some 3,618 nautical miles from the spot where he was abandoned by Christian.

15th January 1790
Christian and the *Bounty* rediscover Pitcairn, which appears in the wrong place on the Royal Navy's charts, and thus offers a good place to evade capture.

23rd January 1790
The mutineers burn the *Bounty*, which sinks off the coast of Pitcairn.

13th March 1790
Bligh arrives back at Portsmouth and reports the mutiny to the Admiralty.

7th November 1790
The Royal Navy dispatches HMS *Pandora* to search for the *Bounty* and capture the mutineers.

23rd March 1791
The *Pandora* reaches Otaheite and the loyalist crew Christian let off there come aboard, arrested as suspected mutineers. The *Pandora*'s crew capture ten more men from the list Bligh provided over the next few weeks.

8th May 1791
The *Pandora* leaves Otaheite.

29th August 1791
The *Pandora* runs aground on the Great Barrier Reef, sinking the next day. Most of the mutineers are released at the last moment, but four (Henry Hillbrandt, Richard Skinner, George Stewart and John Sumner) are killed.

16th September 1791
The survivors from the *Pandora* (including the mutineers) reach Timor in four small launches and then continue their return journey to England.

12th August 1792
The Royal Navy's court martial proceedings begin against ten *Bounty* crewmembers.

18th September 1792

The trial reaches its conclusion. Four men are acquitted (Michael Byrne, Joseph Coleman, Thomas McIntosh and Charles Norman). Two are found guilty but are pardoned (Peter Haywood and James Morrison). Another is reprieved due to a legal technicality and later also pardoned (William Musprat). Three are found guilty (Thomas Burkitt, Thomas Ellison and John Millward). They are sentenced to death.

29th October 1792

Burkitt, Ellison and Millward are hanged (by slow strangulation) aboard HMS *Brunswick* at Spithead.

20th September 1793

Christian and four other mutineers are killed by men who had joined the *Bounty* at Otaheite and settled on Pitcairn with them.

15th May 1794

Christian's brother, the lawyer Edward Christian, publishes his Appendix, which calls into doubt Bligh's account.

3rd December 1794

Bligh publishes his response to Edward Christian.

1808

The first ship to visit Pitcairn since the *Bounty* was sunk finds John Adams is the sole surviving mutineer. The public learns the fates of the other mutineers. Adams receives a pardon in 1825.

FOREWORD
BY PETE GOSS

MY FASCINATION FOR THE MUTINY on the *Bounty* began as a child when my father spun the yarn, featuring wild seamen wielding pistols and cutlasses amongst the Pacific Islands. It drilled its way deep into my imagination. I had never heard of the mutiny before, or the small-boat adventure that followed it. I was hooked.

The sea was always going to be in my blood and as my knowledge and experience of the sea and ships developed so my perception of the mutiny changed. Life is never black and white and the more experience and wisdom one picks up the more shades of grey become apparent. One is better able to relate to the past – the blanks can be filled with empathy.

I did a single-handed transatlantic voyage on a 26ft Firebird catamaran, shivering my way across the North Atlantic as I slept on deck exposed to the elements. On another transatlantic voyage the boat took on a lot of water and all my food was spoiled so that all I had was tea with sugar for the last ten days. I learnt what it was to be hungry, not starving of course but hungry enough to get a sense of what Bligh and his crew must have endured.

As training manager for the British Steel Challenge I was responsible for training everyone in the fleet and played a key role in skipper selection. As such I had an intimate understanding of all the characters across the fleet. The first leg was a disaster for Commercial Union and the crew 'mutinied', in the sense that they had had enough and called for a new skipper, which was duly arranged. What struck me at the time was that the reality was far from the black and white scenario as the press would have had it. It was a complex combination of subtle characters and circumstances that led to the split and I am sure that if the odd individual hadn't been in place the outcome would have been different. The crew went on to a successful circumnavigation and the skipper went to many successful miles.

I have always been fascinated by leadership and spend a lot of my time teaching it in business schools around the world. I myself have had to wrestle with testing decisions from abandoning ship, replacing crew, rescuing a life and being rescued myself.

So it was with a lot more wisdom that I revisited the Bligh story in the edition you have in your hand. I just couldn't put it down. There is a rawness to it that you don't get with many historical books where you are spoon-fed someone else's take on what happened. This one gives you the story from the mouths of those who were actually there.

I found myself alongside the crew of the *Bounty* who remained loyal to Bligh as they undertook what was an incredible voyage of seamanship, navigation and survival – a voyage that was born of a human tragedy which erupted between two strong characters. These characters come to life as their emotions and conflicts ghost between the lines, giving you glimpses of an extraordinary event and the tensions that culminated in mutiny. This book draws you into that drama and allows you to make your own conclusions and observations. It is both compelling and thought provoking.

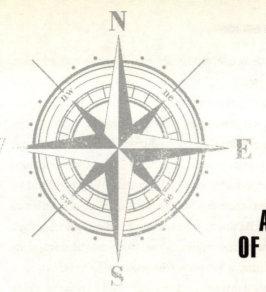

A NARRATIVE OF THE MUTINY

A Narrative of the Mutiny on Board His Majesty's Ship
Bounty and the Subsequent Voyage of Part of the Crew
in the Ship's Boat from Tofoa, one of the Friendly Islands,
to Timor, a Dutch Settlement in the East Indies

by Lieutenant William Bligh

THE FOLLOWING NARRATIVE IS ONLY a part of a voyage undertaken for the purpose of conveying the breadfruit tree from the South Sea Islands to the West Indies. The manner in which this expedition miscarried, with the subsequent transactions and events, are here related. This part of the voyage is not first in the order of time, yet the circumstances are so distinct from that by which it was preceded, that it appears unnecessary to delay giving as much early information as possible concerning so extraordinary an event. The rest will be laid before the public as soon as it can be got ready; and it is intended to publish it in such a manner, as, with the present Narrative, will make the account of the voyage complete.

At present, for the better understanding the following pages, it is sufficient to inform the reader that in August, 1787, I was appointed to command the *Bounty*, a ship of 215 tons burthen, carrying 4 six-pounders, 4 swivels, and 46 men, including myself and every person on board. We sailed from England in December, 1787, and arrived at Otaheite the 26th of October, 1788. On the 4th of April, 1789, we left Otaheite, with every favourable appearance of completing the object of the voyage, in a manner equal to my most sanguine expectations. At this period the ensuing Narrative commences.

April 1789

I sailed from Otaheite on the 4th of April 1789, having on board 1,015 fine breadfruit plants, besides many other valuable fruits of that country, which, with unremitting attention, we had been collecting for three and twenty weeks, and which were now in the highest state of perfection.

On the 11th of April, I discovered an island in latitude 18° 52´ S and longitude 200° 19´ E by the natives called Whytootackee. On the 24th we anchored at Annamooka, one of the Friendly Islands; from which, after completing our wood and water, I sailed on the 27th, having every reason to expect, from the fine condition of the plants, that they would continue healthy.

On the evening of the 28th, owing to light winds, we were not clear of the islands, and at night I directed my course towards Tofoa. The master had the first watch; the gunner the middle watch; and Mr Christian, one of the mates, the morning watch. This was the turn of duty for the night.

Just before sun-rising, Mr Christian, with the master at arms, gunner's mate, and Thomas Burket, seaman, came into my cabin while I was asleep, and seizing me, tied my hands with a cord behind my back, and threatened me with instant death if I spoke or made the least noise: I, however, called so loud as to alarm everyone; but they had already secured the officers who were not of their party, by placing sentinels at their doors. There were three men at my cabin door, besides the four within; Christian had only a cutlass in his hand, the others had muskets and bayonets. I was hauled out of bed, and forced on deck in my shirt, suffering great pain from the tightness with which they had tied my hands. I demanded the reason of such violence, but received no other answer than threats of instant death if I did not hold my tongue. Mr Elphinston, the master's mate, was kept in his berth; Mr Nelson, botanist, Mr Peckover, gunner, Mr Ledward, surgeon, and the master, were confined to their cabins; and also the clerk, Mr Samuel, but he soon obtained leave to come on deck. The fore hatchway was guarded by sentinels; the boatswain and carpenter were, however, allowed to come on deck, where they saw me standing abaft the mizen-mast, with my hands tied behind my back, under a guard, with Christian at their head.

The boatswain was now ordered to hoist the launch out, with a threat, if he did not do it instantly, to take care of himself.

The boat being out, Mr Hayward and Mr Hallet, midshipmen, and Mr Samuel, were ordered into it; upon which I demanded the cause of such an order, and endeavoured to persuade someone to a sense of duty; but it was to no effect: 'Hold your tongue, Sir, or you are dead this instant,' was constantly repeated to me.

The master, by this time, had sent to be allowed to come on deck, which was permitted; but he was soon ordered back again to his cabin.

I continued my endeavours to turn the tide of affairs, when Christian changed the cutlass he had in his hand for a bayonet that was brought to him, and, holding me with a strong grip by the cord that tied my hands, he with many oaths threatened to kill me immediately if I would not be quiet: the villains round me had their pieces cocked and bayonets fixed. Particular people were now called on to go into the boat, and were hurried over the side: whence I concluded that with these people I was to be set adrift.

I therefore made another effort to bring about a change, but with no other effect than to be threatened with having my brains blown out.

The boatswain and seamen, who were to go in the boat, were allowed to collect twine, canvas, lines, sails, cordage, an eight and twenty gallon cask of water, and the carpenter to take his tool chest. Mr Samuel got 150lbs of bread, with a small quantity of rum and wine. He also got a quadrant and compass into the boat; but was forbidden, on pain of death, to touch either map, ephemeris, book of astronomical observations, sextant, time-keeper, or any of my surveys or drawings.

The mutineers now hurried those they meant to get rid of into the boat. When most of them were in, Christian directed a dram to be served to each of his own crew. I now unhappily saw that nothing could be done to effect the recovery of the ship: there was no one to assist me, and every endeavour on my part was answered with threats of death.

The officers were called, and forced over the side into the boat, while I was kept apart from everyone, abaft the mizen-mast; Christian, armed with a bayonet, holding me by the bandage that secured my hands. The guard round me had their pieces cocked, but, on my daring the ungrateful wretches to fire, they uncocked them.

Isaac Martin, one of the guard over me, I saw had an inclination to assist me, and, as he fed me with shaddock, (my lips being quite parched with my endeavours to bring about a change) we explained our wishes to each other by our looks; but this being observed, Martin was instantly removed from me; his inclination then was to leave the ship, for which purpose he got into the boat; but with many threats they obliged him to return.

The armourer, Joseph Coleman, and the two carpenters, McIntosh and Norman, were also kept contrary to their inclination; and they begged of me, after I was astern in the boat, to remember that they declared they had no hand in the transaction. Michael Byrne, I am told, likewise wanted to leave the ship.

It is of no moment for me to recount my endeavours to bring back the offenders to a sense of their duty: all I could do was by speaking to them in general; but my endeavours were of no avail, for I was kept securely bound, and no one but the guard suffered to come near me.

To Mr Samuel I am indebted for securing my journals and commission, with some material ship papers. Without these I had nothing to certify what I had done, and my honour and character might have been suspected, without my possessing a proper document to have defended them. All this he did with great resolution, though guarded and strictly watched. He attempted to save the time-keeper, and a box with all my surveys, drawings, and remarks for fifteen years past, which were numerous; when he was hurried away, with 'Damn your eyes, you are well off to get what you have.'

It appeared to me, that Christian was some time in doubt whether he should keep the carpenter, or his mates; at length he determined on the latter, and the carpenter was ordered into the boat. He was permitted, but not without some opposition, to take his tool chest.

Much altercation took place among the mutinous crew during the whole business: some swore 'I'll be damned if he does not find his way home, if he gets any thing with him' (meaning me); others, when the carpenter's chest was carrying away, 'Damn my eyes, he will have a vessel built in a month.' While others laughed at the helpless situation of the boat, being very deep, and so little room for those who were in her. As for Christian, he seemed meditating instant destruction on himself and everyone.

I asked for arms, but they laughed at me, and said I was well acquainted with the people where I was going, and therefore did not want them; four cutlasses, however, were thrown into the boat, after we were veered astern.

When the officers and men, with whom I was suffered to have no communication, were put into the boat, they only waited for me, and the master at arms informed Christian of it; who then said 'Come, Captain Bligh, your officers and men are now in the boat, and you must go with them; if you attempt to make the least resistance you will instantly be put to death' and, without any farther ceremony, holding me by the cord that tied my hands, with a tribe of armed ruffians about me, I was forced over the side, where they untied my hands. Being in the boat we were veered astern by a rope. A few pieces of pork were then thrown to us, and some clothes, also the cutlasses I have already mentioned; and it was now that the armourer and carpenters called out to me to remember that they had no hand in the transaction. After having undergone a great deal of ridicule, and been kept some time to make sport for these unfeeling wretches, we were at length cast adrift in the open ocean.

I had with me in the boat the following persons:

Names	Stations
John Fryer	Master
Thomas Ledward	Acting Surgeon
David Nelson	Botanist
William Peckover	Gunner
William Cole	Boatswain
William Purcell	Carpenter
William Elphinston	Master's Mate
Thomas Hayward } John Hallett	Midshipmen
John Norton } Peter Linkletter	Quarter Masters
Lawrence Lebogue	Sailmaker
John Smith } Thomas Hall	Cooks
George Simpson	Quarter Master's Mate
Robert Tinkler	A boy
Robert Lamb	Butcher
Mr Samuel	Clerk

There remained on board the *Bounty*, as pirates:

Fletcher Christian	Master's Mate
Peter Haywood	
Edward Young	Midshipmen
George Stewart	
Charles Churchill	Master at Arms
John Mills	Gunner's Mate
James Morrison	Boatswain's Mate
Thomas Burkitt	Able Seaman
Matthew Quintal	Ditto
John Sumner	Ditto
John Millward	Ditto
William M'koy	Ditto
Henry Hillbrant	Ditto
Michael Byrne	Ditto
William Musprat	Ditto
Alexander Smith	Ditto
John Williams	Ditto
Thomas Ellison	Ditto
Isaac Martin	Ditto
Richard Skinner	Ditto
Matthew Thompson	Ditto
William Brown	Gardener
Joseph Coleman	Armourer
Charles Norman	Carpenter's Mate
Thomas McIntosh	Carpenter's Crew

In all 25 hands, and the most able men of the ship's company.

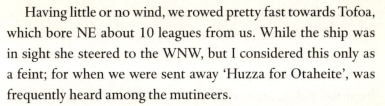

Having little or no wind, we rowed pretty fast towards Tofoa, which bore NE about 10 leagues from us. While the ship was in sight she steered to the WNW, but I considered this only as a feint; for when we were sent away 'Huzza for Otaheite', was frequently heard among the mutineers.

Christian, the captain of the gang, is of a respectable family in the north of England. This was the third voyage he had made with me; and, as I found it necessary to keep my ship's company at three watches, I gave him an order to take charge of the third, his abilities being thoroughly equal to the task; and by this means my master and gunner were not at watch and watch.

Haywood is also of a respectable family in the north of England, and a young man of abilities, as well as Christian. These two were objects of my particular regard and attention, and I took great pains to instruct them, for they really promised, as professional men, to be a credit to their country.

Young was well recommended, and appeared to me an able stout seaman; therefore I was glad to take him: he, however, fell short of what his appearance promised.

Stewart was a young man of creditable parents, in the Orkneys; at which place, on the return of the *Resolution* from the South Seas, in 1780, we received so many civilities, that, on that account only, I should gladly have taken him with me: but, independent of this recommendation, he was a seaman, and had always borne a good character.

Notwithstanding the roughness with which I was treated, the remembrance of past kindnesses produced some signs of remorse in Christian. When they were forcing me out of the ship, I asked him if this treatment was a proper return for the many instances he had received of my friendship? He appeared disturbed at my question, and answered, with much emotion, 'That, Captain Bligh, that is the thing; I am in hell – I am in hell.'

As soon as I had time to reflect, I felt an inward satisfaction which prevented any depression of my spirits: conscious of my integrity, and anxious solicitude for the good of the service in which I was engaged, I found my mind wonderfully supported, and I began to conceive hopes, notwithstanding so heavy a calamity, that I should one day be able to account to my King and country for the misfortune.

A few hours before, my situation had been peculiarly flattering. I had a ship in the most perfect order, and well stored with every necessary both for service and health: by early attention to those particulars I had, as much as lay in my power, provided against any accident, in case I could not get through Endeavour Straits, as well as against what might befall me in them; add to this, the plants had been successfully preserved in the most flourishing state: so that, upon the whole, the voyage was two thirds completed, and the remaining part in a very promising way; every person on board being in perfect health, to establish which was ever amongst the principal objects of my attention.

It will very naturally be asked, what could be the reason for such a revolt? In answer to which, I can only conjecture that the mutineers had assured themselves of a more happy life among the Otaheiteans, than they could possibly have in England; which, joined to some female connections, have most probably been the principal cause of the whole transaction.

The women at Otaheite are handsome, mild and cheerful in their manners and conversation, possessed of great sensibility, and have sufficient delicacy to make them admired and beloved.

The chiefs were so much attached to our people, that they rather encouraged their stay among them than otherwise, and even made them promises of large possessions. Under these, and many other attendant circumstances, equally desirable, it is now perhaps not so much to be wondered at, though scarcely possible to have been foreseen, that a set of sailors, most of them void of connections, should be led away; especially when, in addition to such powerful inducements, they imagined it in their power to fix themselves in the midst of plenty, on the finest island in the world, where they need not labour, and where the allurements of dissipation are beyond anything that can be conceived. The utmost, however, that any commander could have supposed to have happened is that some of the people would have been tempted to desert. But if it should be asserted, that a commander is to guard against an act of mutiny and piracy in his own ship, more than by the common rules of service, it is as much as to say that he must sleep locked up, and when awake, be girded with pistols.

Desertions have happened, more or less, from many of the ships that have been at the Society Islands; but it ever has been in the commander's power to make the chiefs return their people: the knowledge, therefore, that it was unsafe to desert, perhaps, first led mine to consider with what ease so small a ship might be surprised, and that so favourable an opportunity would never offer to them again.

The secrecy of this mutiny is beyond all conception. Thirteen of the party, who were with me, had always lived forward among the people; yet neither they, nor the messmates of Christian, Stewart, Haywood, and Young, had ever observed any circumstance to give them suspicion of what was going on. With such close-planned acts of villainy, and my mind free from any suspicion, it is not wonderful that I have been got the better of. Perhaps, if I had had marines, a sentinel at my cabin-door might have prevented it; for I slept with the door always open, that the officer of the watch might have access to me on all occasions. The possibility of such a conspiracy was ever the farthest from my thoughts. Had their mutiny been occasioned by any grievances, either real or imaginary, I must have discovered symptoms of their discontent, which would have put me on my guard but the case was far otherwise. Christian in particular I was on the most friendly terms with; that very day he was engaged to have dined with me; and the preceding night he excused himself from supping with me, on pretence of being unwell; for which I felt concerned, having no suspicions of his integrity and honour.

It now remained with me to consider what was best to be done. My first determination was to seek a supply of breadfruit and water at Tofoa, and afterwards to sail for Tongataboo; and there risk a solicitation to Poulaho, the king, to equip my boat, and grant a supply of water and provisions, so as to enable us to reach the East Indies.

The quantity of provisions I found in the boat was 150 lb of bread, 16 pieces of pork, each piece weighing 2 lb 6 quarts of rum, 6 bottles of wine, with 28 gallons of water, and four empty barrecoes.

Wednesday 29th April

(It is to be observed that the account of time is kept in the nautical way, each day ending at noon. Thus the beginning of the 29th of April is, according to the common way of reckoning, the afternoon of the 28th.)

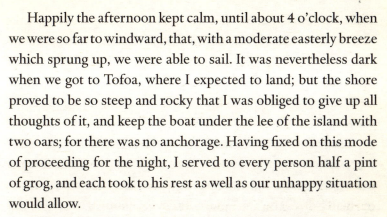

Happily the afternoon kept calm, until about 4 o'clock, when we were so far to windward, that, with a moderate easterly breeze which sprung up, we were able to sail. It was nevertheless dark when we got to Tofoa, where I expected to land; but the shore proved to be so steep and rocky that I was obliged to give up all thoughts of it, and keep the boat under the lee of the island with two oars; for there was no anchorage. Having fixed on this mode of proceeding for the night, I served to every person half a pint of grog, and each took to his rest as well as our unhappy situation would allow.

In the morning, at dawn of day, we set off along shore in search of landing, and about 10 o'clock we discovered a stony cove at the NW part of the island, where I dropped the grapnel within 20 yards of the rocks. A great deal of surf ran on the shore; but, as I was unwilling to diminish our stock of provisions, I landed Mr Samuel and some others, who climbed the cliffs, and got into the country to search for supplies. The rest of us remained at the cove, not discovering any way to get into the country, but that by which Mr Samuel had proceeded. It was great consolation to me to find, that the spirits of my people did not sink, notwithstanding our miserable and almost hopeless situation. Towards noon Mr Samuel returned, with a few quarts of water, which he had found in holes; but he had met with no spring or any prospect of a sufficient supply in that particular, and had only seen signs of inhabitants. As it was impossible to know how much we might be in want, I only issued a morsel of bread, and a glass of wine, to each person for dinner.

I observed the latitude of this cove to be 19° 41′ S.

This is the NW part of Tofoa, the north-westernmost of the Friendly Islands.

Thursday 30th April

Fair weather, but the wind blew so violently from the ESE that I could not venture to sea. Our detention therefore made it absolutely necessary to see what we could do more for our support; for I determined, if possible, to keep my first stock entire: I therefore weighed, and rowed along shore, to see if anything could be got; and at last discovered some coconut trees, but they were on the top of high precipices, and the surf made it dangerous landing; both one and the other we, however, got the better of. Some, with much difficulty, climbed the cliffs, and got about 20 coconuts, and others slung them to ropes, by which we hauled them through the surf into the boat. This was all that could be done here; and, as I found no place so eligible as the one we had left to spend the night at, I returned to the cove and, having served a coconut to each person, we went to rest again in the boat.

At dawn of day I attempted to get to sea; but the wind and weather proved so bad, that I was glad to return to my former station; where, after issuing a morsel of bread and a spoonful of rum to each person, we landed, and I went off with Mr Nelson, Mr Samuel, and some others, into the country, having hauled ourselves up the precipice by long vines, which were fixed there by the natives for that purpose; this being the only way into the country.

We found a few deserted huts, and a small plantain walk, but little taken care of; from which we could only collect three small bunches of plantains. After passing this place, we came to a deep gully that led towards a mountain, near a volcano; and, as I conceived that in the rainy season very great torrents of water must pass through it, we hoped to find sufficient for our use remaining in some holes of the rocks; but, after all our search, the whole that we found was only 9 gallons, in the course of the day. We advanced within two miles of the foot of the highest mountain in the island, on which is the volcano that is almost constantly burning. The country near it is all covered with lava, and has a most dreary appearance. As we had not been fortunate in our discoveries, and saw but little to alleviate our distresses, we filled our coconut shells with the water we found, and returned exceedingly fatigued and faint. When I came to the precipice whence we were to descend into the cove, I was seized with such a dizziness in my head, that I thought it scarce possible to effect it: however, by the assistance of Mr Nelson, and others, they at last got me down, in a weak condition. Every person being returned by noon, I gave about an ounce of pork and two plantains to each, with half a glass of wine. I again observed the latitude of this place 19° 41′ S. The people who remained by the boat I had directed to look for fish, or what they could pick up about the rocks; but nothing eatable could be found: so that, upon the whole, we considered ourselves on as miserable a spot of land as could well be imagined.

I could not say positively, from the former knowledge I had of this island, whether it was inhabited or not; but I knew it was considered inferior to the other islands, and I was not certain but that the Indians only resorted to it at particular times. I was very anxious to ascertain this point; for, in case there had only been a few people here, and those could have furnished us with but very moderate supplies, the remaining in this spot to have made preparations for our voyage, would have been preferable to the risk of going amongst multitudes, where perhaps we might lose everything. A party, therefore, sufficiently strong, I determined should go another route, as soon as the sun became lower; and they cheerfully undertook it.

Friday 1st May
Stormy weather, wind ESE and SE. About 2 o'clock in the afternoon the party set out; but, after suffering much fatigue, they returned in the evening, without any kind of success.

At the head of the cove, about 150 yards from the waterside, was a cave; across the stony beach was about 100 yards, and the only way from the country into the cove was that which I have already described. The situation secured us from the danger of being surprised, and I determined to remain on shore for the night, with a part of my people, that the others might have more room to rest in the boat with the master; whom I directed to lie at a grapnel, and be watchful, in case we should be attacked. I ordered one plantain for each person to be boiled; and, having supped on this scanty allowance, with a quarter of a pint of grog, and fixed the watches for the night, those whose turn it was, laid down to sleep in the cave; before which we kept up a good fire, yet notwithstanding we were much troubled with flies and mosquitoes.

At dawn of day the party set out again in a different route, to see what they could find; in the course of which they suffered greatly for want of water: they, however, met with two men, a woman, and a child; the men came with them to the cove, and brought two coconut shells of water. I immediately made friends with these people, and sent them away for breadfruit, plantains, and water. Soon after other natives came to us; and by noon I had 30 of them about me, trading with the articles we were in want of: but I could only afford one ounce of pork, and a quarter of a breadfruit, to each man for dinner, with half a pint of water; for I was fixed in not using any of the bread or water in the boat.

No particular chief was yet among the natives: they were, notwithstanding, tractable, and behaved honestly, giving the provisions they brought for a few buttons and beads. The party who had been out, informed me of having discovered several neat plantations; so that it became no longer a doubt of there being settled inhabitants on the island; and for that reason I determined to get what I could, and sail the first moment the wind and weather would allow me to put to sea.

Saturday 2nd May

Stormy weather, wind ESE. It had hitherto been a weighty consideration with me, how I was to account to the natives for the loss of my ship: I knew they had too much sense to be amused with a story that the ship was to join me, when she was not in sight from the hills. I was at first doubtful whether I should tell the real fact, or say that the ship had overset and sunk, and that only we were saved: the latter appeared to me to be the most proper and advantageous to us, and I accordingly instructed my people, that we might all agree in one story. As I expected, enquiries were made after the ship, and they seemed readily satisfied with our account; but there did not appear the least symptom of joy or sorrow in their faces, although I fancied I discovered some marks of surprise. Some of the natives were coming and going the whole afternoon, and we got enough of breadfruit, plantains, and coconuts for another day; but water they only brought us about five pints. A canoe also came in with four men, and brought a few coconuts and breadfruit, which I bought as I had done the rest. Nails were much enquired after, but I would not suffer one to be shewn, as I wanted them for the use of the boat.

Towards evening I had the satisfaction to find our stock of provisions somewhat increased: but the natives did not appear to have much to spare. What they brought was in such small quantities, that I had no reason to hope we should be able to procure from them sufficient to stock us for our voyage. At sunset all the natives left us in quiet possession of the cove. I thought this a good sign, and made no doubt that they would come again the next day with a larger proportion of food and water, with which I hoped to sail without farther delay: for if, in attempting to get to Tongataboo, we should be blown away from the islands altogether, there would be a larger quantity of provisions to support us against such a misfortune.

At night I served a quarter of a breadfruit and a coconut to each person for supper; and, a good fire being made, all but the watch went to sleep.

At daybreak I was happy to find everyone's spirits a little revived, and that they no longer regarded me with those anxious looks, which had constantly been directed towards me since we lost sight of the ship: every countenance appeared to have a degree of cheerfulness, and they all seemed determined to do their best.

As I doubted of water being brought by the natives, I sent a party among the gullies in the mountains, with empty shells, to see what they could get. In their absence the natives came about us, as I expected, but more numerous; also two canoes came in from round the north side of the island. In one of them was an elderly chief, called Maccaackavow. Soon after some of our foraging party returned, and with them came a good-looking chief, called Eegijeefow, or perhaps more properly Eefow, Egij or Eghee, signifying a chief. To both these men I made a present of an old shirt and a knife, and I soon found they either had seen me, or had heard of my being at Annamooka. They knew I had been with Captain Cook, who they enquired after, and also Captain Clerk. They were very inquisitive to know in what manner I had lost my ship. During this conversation a young man appeared, whom I remembered to have seen at Annamooka, called Nageete: he expressed much pleasure at seeing me. I now enquired after Poulaho and Feenow, who, they said, were at Tongataboo; and Eefow agreed to accompany me thither, if I would wait till the weather moderated. The readiness and affability of this man gave me much satisfaction.

This, however, was but of short duration, for the natives began to increase in number, and I observed some symptoms of a design against us; soon after they attempted to haul the boat on shore, when I threatened Eefow with a cutlass, to induce him to make them desist; which they did, and everything became quiet again. My people, who had been in the mountains, now returned with about 3 gallons of water. I kept buying up the little breadfruit that was brought to us, and likewise some spears to arm my men with, having only four cutlasses, two of which were in the boat. As we had no means of improving our situation, I told our people I would wait until sunset, by which time, perhaps, something might happen in our favour: that if we attempted to go at present, we must fight our way through, which we could do more advantageously at night; and that in the mean time we would endeavour to get off to the boat what we had bought. The beach was now lined with the natives, and we heard nothing but the knocking of stones together, which they had in each hand. I knew very well this was the sign of an attack. It being now noon, I served a coconut and a breadfruit to each person for dinner, and gave some to the chiefs, with whom I continued to appear intimate and friendly. They frequently importuned me to sit down, but I as constantly refused; for it occurred both to Mr Nelson and myself, that they intended to seize hold of me, if I gave them such an opportunity. Keeping, therefore, constantly on our guard, we were suffered to eat our uncomfortable meal in some quietness.

Sunday 3rd May
Fresh gales at SE and ESE, varying to the NE in the latter part, with a storm of wind.

After dinner we began by little and little to get our things into the boat, which was a troublesome business, on account of the surf. I carefully watched the motions of the natives, who still increased in number, and found that, instead of their intention being to leave us, fires were made, and places fixed on for their stay during the night. Consultations were also held among them, and everything assured me we should be attacked. I sent orders to the master that when he saw us coming down he should keep the boat close to the shore, that we might the more readily embark.

I had my journal on shore with me, writing the occurrences in the cave, and in sending it down to the boat it was nearly snatched away, but for the timely assistance of the gunner.

The sun was near setting when I gave the word, on which every person who was on shore with me boldly took up his proportion of things, and carried them to the boat. The chiefs asked me if I

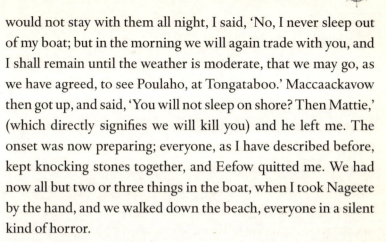

would not stay with them all night, I said, 'No, I never sleep out of my boat; but in the morning we will again trade with you, and I shall remain until the weather is moderate, that we may go, as we have agreed, to see Poulaho, at Tongataboo.' Maccaackavow then got up, and said, 'You will not sleep on shore? Then Mattie,' (which directly signifies we will kill you) and he left me. The onset was now preparing; everyone, as I have described before, kept knocking stones together, and Eefow quitted me. We had now all but two or three things in the boat, when I took Nageete by the hand, and we walked down the beach, everyone in a silent kind of horror.

When I came to the boat, and was seeing the people embark, Nageete wanted me to stay to speak to Eefow; but I found he was encouraging them to the attack, and I determined, had it then begun, to have killed him for his treacherous behaviour. I ordered the carpenter not to quit me until the other people were in the boat. Nageete, finding I would not stay, loosed himself from my hold and went off, and we all got into the boat except one man, who, while I was getting on board, quitted it, and ran up the beach to cast the stern fast off, notwithstanding the master and others called to him to return while they were hauling me out of the water.

I was no sooner in the boat than the attack began by about 200 men; the unfortunate poor man who had run up the beach was knocked down, and the stones flew like a shower of shot. Many Indians got hold of the stern rope, and were near hauling us on shore, and would certainly have done it if I had not had a knife in my pocket, with which I cut the rope. We then hauled off to the grapnel, everyone being more or less hurt. At this time I saw five of the natives about the poor man they had killed, and two of them were beating him about the head with stones in their hands.

We had no time to reflect before, to my surprise, they filled their canoes with stones, and twelve men came off after us to renew the attack, which they did so effectually as nearly to disable all of us. Our grapnel was foul, but Providence here assisted us; the fluke broke, and we got to our oars, and pulled to sea. They, however, could paddle round us, so that we were obliged to sustain the attack without being able to return it, except with such stones as lodged in the boat, and in this I found we were very inferior to them. We could not close because our boat was lumbered and heavy, and that they knew very well: I therefore adopted the expedient of throwing overboard some clothes, which they lost time in picking up; and, as it was now almost dark, they gave over the attack, and returned towards the shore, leaving us to reflect on our unhappy situation.

The poor man I lost was John Norton: this was his second voyage with me as a quarter-master, and his worthy character made me lament his loss very much. He has left an aged parent, I am told, whom he supported.

I once before sustained an attack of a similar nature, with a smaller number of Europeans, against a multitude of Indians; it was after the death of Captain Cook, on the Morai at Owhyhee, where I was left by Lieutenant King: yet, notwithstanding, I did not conceive that the power of a man's arm could throw stones, from 2 to 8 lb weight, with such force and exactness as these people did. Here unhappily I was without arms, and the Indians knew it; but it was a fortunate circumstance that they did not begin to attack us in the cave: in that case our destruction must have been inevitable, and we should have had nothing left for it but to die as bravely as we could, fighting close together; in which I found everyone cheerfully disposed to join me. This appearance of resolution deterred them, supposing they could effect their purpose without risk after we were in the boat.

Taking this as a sample of the dispositions of the Indians, there was little reason to expect much benefit if I persevered in my intention of visiting Poulaho; for I considered their good behaviour hitherto to proceed from a dread of our firearms, which, now knowing us destitute of, would cease; and, even supposing our lives not in danger, the boat and everything we had would most probably be taken from us, and thereby all hopes precluded of ever being able to return to our native country.

We were now sailing along the west side of the island Tofoa, and my mind was employed in considering what was best to be done, when I was solicited by all hands to take them towards home: and, when I told them no hopes of relief for us remained, but what I might find at New Holland, until I came to Timor, a distance of full 1,200 leagues, where was a Dutch settlement, but in what part of the island I knew not, they all agreed to live on one ounce of bread, and a quarter of a pint of water per day. Therefore, after examining our stock of provisions, and recommending this as a sacred promise for ever to their memory, we bore away across a sea, where the navigation is but little known, in a small boat, twenty-three feet long from stern to stern, deep laden with eighteen men; without a chart, and nothing but my own recollection and general knowledge of the situation of places, assisted by a book of latitudes and longitudes, to guide us. I was happy, however, to see everyone better satisfied with our situation in this particular than myself.

Our stock of provisions consisted of about 150 lb of bread, 28 gallons of water, 20 pounds of pork, three bottles of wine, and five quarts of rum. The difference between this and the quantity we had on leaving the ship was principally owing to loss in the bustle and confusion of the attack. A few coconuts were in the boat, and some breadfruit, but the latter was trampled to pieces.

It was about 8 o'clock at night when I bore away under a reefed lug fore-sail: and, having divided the people into watches, and got the boat in a little order, we returned God thanks for our miraculous preservation, and, fully confident of His gracious support, I found my mind more at ease than for some time past.

At daybreak the gale increased; the sun rose very fiery and red, a sure indication of a severe gale of wind. At eight it blew a violent storm, and the sea ran very high, so that between the seas the sail was becalmed, and when on the top of the sea it was too much to have set: but I was obliged to carry to it, for we were now in very imminent danger and distress, the sea curling over the stern of the boat, which obliged us to bail with all our might. A situation more distressing has, perhaps, seldom been experienced.

Our bread was in bags, and in danger of being spoiled by the wet: to be starved to death was inevitable, if this could not be prevented: I therefore began to examine what clothes there were in the boat, and what other things could be spared; and, having determined that only two suits should be kept for each person, the rest was thrown overboard, with some rope and spare sails, which lightened the boat considerably, and we had more room to bail the water out. Fortunately the carpenter had a good chest in the boat, into which I put the bread the first favourable moment. His tool chest also was cleared, and the tools stowed in the bottom of the boat, so that this became a second convenience.

I now served a teaspoonful of rum to each person (for we were very wet and cold) with a quarter of a breadfruit, which was scarce eatable, for dinner; but our engagement was now strictly to be carried into execution, and I was fully determined to make what provisions I had last eight weeks, let the daily proportion be ever so small.

At noon I considered my course and distance from Tofoa to be WNW 3/4 W 86 miles, my latitude 19° 27´ S. I directed my course to the WNW, that I might get a sight of the islands called Feejee, if they laid in the direction the natives had pointed out to me.

Monday 4th May

This day the weather was very severe, it blew a storm from NE to ESE. The sea ran higher than yesterday, and the fatigue of bailing, to keep the boat from filling, was exceedingly great. We could do nothing more than keep before the sea; in the course of which the boat performed so wonderfully well, that I no longer dreaded any danger in that respect. But among the hardships we were to undergo, that of being constantly wet was not the least: the nights were very cold, and at daylight our limbs were so benumbed, that we could scarce find the use of them. At this time I served a teaspoonful of rum to each person, which we all found great benefit from.

As I have mentioned before, I determined to keep to the WNW, until I got more to the northward, for I not only expected to have better weather, but to see the Feejee Islands, as I have often understood, from the natives of Annamooka, that they lie in that direction; Captain Cook likewise considers them to be NW by W from Tongataboo. Just before noon we discovered a small flat island of a moderate height, bearing WSW, 4 or 5 leagues. I observed in latitude 18° 58′ S; our longitude, by account, 3° 4′ W from the island Tofoa, having made a N 72° W course, distance 95 miles, since yesterday noon. I divided five small coconuts for our dinner, and everyone was satisfied.

Tuesday 5th May
Towards the evening the gale considerably abated. Wind SE.

A little after noon, other islands appeared, and at a quarter past 3 o'clock we could count eight, bearing from S round by the west to NW by N; those to the south, which were the nearest, being 4 leagues distant from us.

I kept my course to the NW by W, between the islands, and at 6 o'clock discovered three other small islands to the NW, the westernmost of them bore NW 1/2 W 7 leagues. I steered to the southward of these islands, a WNW course for the night, under a reefed sail.

Served a few broken pieces of breadfruit for supper and performed prayers.

The night turned out fair, and, having had tolerable rest, everyone seemed considerably better in the morning, and contentedly breakfasted on a few pieces of yams that were found in the boat. After breakfast we prepared a chest for our bread, and it got secured: but unfortunately a great deal was damaged and rotten; this nevertheless we were glad to keep for use.

I had hitherto been scarcely able to keep any account of our run; but we now equipped ourselves a little better, by getting a log-line marked, and, having practised at counting seconds; several could do it with some degree of exactness.

The islands I have passed lie between the latitude of 19° 5′ S and 18° 19′ S, and, according to my reckoning, from 3° 17′ to 3° 46′ W longitude from the island Tofoa: the largest may be about 6 leagues in circuit; but it is impossible for me to be very exact. To show where they are to be found again is the most my situation enabled me to do. The sketch I have made will give a comparative view of their extent. I believe all the larger islands are inhabited, as they appeared very fertile.

At noon I observed, in latitude 18° 10′ S, and considered my course and distance from yesterday noon, NW by W 1/2 W, 94 miles; longitude, by account, from Tofoa 4° 29′ W.

For dinner, I served some of the damaged bread, and a quarter of a pint of water.

Wednesday 6th May
Fresh breezes ENE, and fair weather, but very hazy.

About 6 o'clock this afternoon I discovered two islands, one bearing W by S 6 leagues, and the other NW by N 8 leagues; I kept to windward of the northernmost, and passing it by 10 o'clock, I resumed my course to the NW and WNW. At daylight in the morning I discovered a number of other islands from SSE to the W, and round to NE by E; between those in the NW I determined to pass. At noon a small sandy island or key, 2 miles distant from me, bore from E to S 3/4 W. I had passed ten islands, the largest of which may be 6 or 8 leagues in circuit. Much larger lands appeared in the SW and N by W, between which I directed my course. Latitude observed 17° 17′ S; course since yesterday noon N 50° W; distance 84 miles; longitude made, by account, 5° 37′ W.

Our supper, breakfast, and dinner, consisted of a quarter of a pint of coconut milk, and the meat, which did not exceed two ounces to each person: it was received very contentedly, but we suffered great drought. I dared not to land, as we had no arms, and were less capable to defend ourselves than we were at Tofoa.

To keep an account of the boat's run was rendered difficult, from being constantly wet with the sea breaking over us; but, as we advanced towards the land, the sea became smoother, and I was enabled to form a sketch of the islands, which will serve to give a general knowledge of their extent. Those I have been near are fruitful and hilly, some very mountainous, and all of a good height.

To our great joy we hooked a fish, but we were miserably disappointed by its being lost in getting into the boat.

Thursday 7th May

Variable weather and cloudy, wind north-easterly, and calms. I continued my course to the NW, between the islands, which, by the evening, appeared of considerable extent, woody and mountainous. At sunset the southernmost bore from S to SW by W, and the northernmost from N by W 1/2 W to NE 1/2 E. At 6 o'clock I was nearly mid-way between them, and about 6 leagues distant from each shore, when I fell in with a coral bank, where I had only four feet water, without the least break on it, or ruffle of the sea to give us warning. I could only see that it extended about a mile on each side of us; but, as it is probable that it extends much farther, I have laid it down so in my sketch.

I now directed my course W by N for the night, and served to each person an ounce of the damaged bread, and a quarter of a pint of water, for supper.

It may readily be supposed, that our lodgings were very miserable and confined, and I had only in my power to remedy the latter defect by putting ourselves at watch and watch; so that one half always sat up while the other lay down on the boat's bottom, or upon a chest, with nothing to cover us but the heavens. Our limbs were dreadfully cramped, for we could not stretch them out, and the nights were so cold, and we so constantly wet, that after a few hours' sleep we could scarce move.

At dawn of day we again discovered land from WSW to WNW, and another island NNW, the latter a high round lump of but little extent; and I could see the southern land that I had passed in the night. Being very wet and cold, I served a spoonful of rum and a morsel of bread for breakfast.

As I advanced towards the land in the west, it appeared in a variety of forms; some extraordinary high rocks, and the country agreeably interspersed with high and low land, covered in some places with wood. Off the NE part lay two small rocky islands, between which and the island to the NE, 4 leagues apart, I directed my course; but a lee current very unexpectedly set us very near to the shore, and I could only get clear of it by rowing, passing close to the reef that surrounded the rocky isles. We now observed two large sailing canoes coming swiftly after us along shore, and, being apprehensive of their intentions, we rowed with some anxiety, being sensible of our weak and defenceless state. It was now noon, calm and cloudy weather, my latitude was therefore doubtful to 3 or 4 miles; my course since yesterday noon N 56 W, distance 79 miles; latitude by account, 16° 29′ S, and longitude by account, from Tofoa, 6° 46´ W. Being constantly wet, it was with the utmost difficulty I could open a book to write, and I am sensible that what I have done can only serve to point out where these lands are to be found again, and give an idea of their extent.

Friday 8th May

All the afternoon the weather was very rainy, attended with thunder and lightning. Wind NNE.

Only one of the canoes gained upon us, and by 3 o'clock in the afternoon was not more than two miles off, when she gave over chase.

If I may judge from the sail of the vessels, they are the same as at the Friendly Islands, and the nearness of their situation leaves little room to doubt of their being the same kind of people. Whether these canoes had any hostile intention against us is a matter of doubt; perhaps we might have benefited by an intercourse with them, but in our defenceless situation it would have been risking too much to make the experiment.

I imagine these to be the islands called Feejee, as their extent, direction, and distance from the Friendly Islands, answers to the description given of them by those Islanders. Heavy rain came on at 4 o'clock, when every person did their utmost to catch some water, and we increased our stock to 34 gallons, besides quenching our thirst for the first time since we had been at sea; but an attendant consequence made us pass the night very miserably, for, being extremely wet, and no dry things to shift or cover us, we experienced cold and shiverings scarce to be conceived. Most fortunately for us, the forenoon turned out fair, and we stripped and dried our clothes. The allowance I issued today was an ounce and a half of pork, a teaspoonful of rum, half a pint of coconut milk, and an ounce of bread. The rum, though so small in quantity, was of the greatest service. A fishing-line was generally towing, and we saw great numbers of fish, but could never catch one.

At noon, I observed, in latitude 16° 4′ S, and found I had made a course, from yesterday noon, N 62° W, distance 62 miles; longitude, by account, from Tofoa, 7° 42′ W.

The land I passed yesterday, and the day before, is a group of islands, 14 or 16 in number, lying between the latitude of 16° 26′ S and 17° 57′ S, and in longitude, by my account, 4° 47′ to 7° 17′ W from Tofoa; three of these islands are very large, having from 30 to 40 leagues of sea-coast.

Saturday 9th May
Fine weather, and light winds from the NE to E by S.

This afternoon we cleaned out the boat, and it employed us till sunset to get everything dry and in order. Hitherto I had issued the allowance by guess, but I now got a pair of scales, made with two coconut shells; and, having accidentally some pistol-balls in the boat, 25 of which weighed one pound, or 16 ounces (it weighed 272 grains), I adopted one, as the proportion of weight that each person should receive of bread at the times I served it. I also amused all hands with describing the situation of New Guinea and New Holland, and gave them every information in my power, that in case any accident happened to me, those who survived might have some idea of what they were about, and be able to find their way to Timor, which at present they knew nothing of, more than the name, and some not that.

At night I served a quarter of a pint of water, and half an ounce of bread, for supper. In the morning, a quarter of a pint of coconut milk, and some of the decayed bread, for breakfast; and for dinner, I divided the meat of four coconuts, with the remainder of the rotten bread, which was only eatable by such distressed people.

At noon, I observed the latitude to be 15° 47′ S; course since yesterday N 75° W; distant 64 miles; longitude made, by account, 8° 45′ W.

Sunday 10th May

The first part of this day fine weather; but after sunset it became squally, with hard rain, thunder, and lightning, and a fresh gale; wind E by S, SE, and SSE.

In the afternoon I got fitted a pair of shrouds for each mast and contrived a canvass weather cloth round the boat, and raised the quarters about nine inches, by nailing on the seats of the stern sheets, which proved of great benefit to us.

About 9 o'clock in the evening the clouds began to gather, and we had a prodigious fall of rain, with severe thunder and lightning. By midnight we had caught about 20 gallons of water. Being miserably wet and cold, I served to each person a teaspoonful of rum, to enable them to bear with their distressed situation. The weather continued extremely bad, and the wind increased; we spent a very miserable night, without sleep, but such as could be got in the midst of rain. The day brought us no relief but its light. The sea was constantly breaking over us, which kept two persons bailing; and we had no choice how to steer, for we were obliged to keep before the waves to avoid filling the boat.

The allowance which I now regularly served to each person was one 25th of a pound of bread, and a quarter of a pint of water, at sunset, eight in the morning, and at noon. Today I gave about half an ounce of pork for dinner, which, though any moderate person would have considered but a mouthful, was divided into three or four.

The rain abated towards noon, and I observed the latitude to be 15° 17′ S; course N 67° W; distance 78 miles; longitude made 10° W.

Monday 11th May

Strong gales from SSE to SE, and very squally weather, with a high breaking sea, so that we were miserably wet, and suffered great cold in the night. In the morning at daybreak I served to every person a teaspoonful of rum, our limbs being so cramped that we could scarce feel the use of them. Our situation was now extremely dangerous, the sea frequently running over our stern, which kept us bailing with all our strength.

At noon the sun appeared, which gave us as much pleasure as in a winter's day in England. I issued the 25th of a pound of bread, and a quarter of a pint of water, as yesterday. Latitude observed 14° 50′ S; course N 71° W; distance 102 miles; and longitude, by account, 11° 39′ W from Tofoa.

Tuesday 12th May

Strong gales at SE, with much rain and dark dismal weather, moderating towards noon and wind varying to the NE.

Having again experienced a dreadful night, the day showed to me a poor miserable set of beings full of wants, without any thing to relieve them. Some complained of a great pain in their bowels, and all of having but very little use of their limbs. What sleep we got was scarce refreshing, we being covered with sea and rain. Two persons were obliged to be always bailing the water out of the boat. I served a spoonful of rum at day-dawn, and the usual allowance of bread and water, for supper, breakfast, and dinner.

At noon it was almost calm, no sun to be seen, and some of us shivering with cold. Course since yesterday W by N; distance 89 miles; latitude, by account, 14° 33′ S; longitude made 13° 9′ W. The direction of my course is to pass to the northward of the New Hebrides.

Wednesday 13th May

Very squally weather, wind southerly. As I saw no prospect of getting our clothes dried, I recommended it to everyone to strip, and wring them through the salt water, by which means they received a warmth, that, while wet with rain, they could not have, and we were less liable to suffer from colds or rheumatic complaints.

In the afternoon we saw a kind of fruit on the water, which Mr Nelson knew to be the Barringtonia of Forster, and, as I saw the same again in the morning, and some men of war birds, I was led to believe we were not far from land.

We continued constantly shipping seas, and bailing, and were very wet and cold in the night; but I could not afford the allowance of rum at daybreak. The 25th of a pound of bread, and water I served as usual. At noon I had a sight of the sun, latitude 14° 17′ S; course W by N 79 miles; longitude made 14° 28′ W.

Thursday 14th May

Fresh breezes and cloudy weather, wind southerly. Constantly shipping water, and very wet, suffering much cold and shiverings in the night. Served the usual allowance of bread and water, three times a day.

At six in the morning, we saw land, from SW by S 8 leagues, to NW by W 3/4 W 6 leagues, which I soon after found to be four islands, all of them high and remarkable. At noon discovered a rocky island NW by N 4 leagues, and another island W 8 leagues, so that the whole were six in number; the four I had first seen bearing from S 1/2 E to SW by S; our distance 3 leagues from the nearest island. My latitude observed was 13° 29′ S, and longitude, by account, from Tofoa, 15° 49′ W; course since yesterday noon N 63° W; distance 89 miles.

Friday 15th May

Fresh gales at SE, and gloomy weather with rain, and a very high sea; two people constantly employed bailing.

At four in the afternoon I passed the westernmost island. At one in the morning I discovered another, bearing WNW, 5 leagues distance, and at 8 o'clock I saw it for the last time, bearing NE 7 leagues. A number of gannets, boobies, and men of war birds were seen.

These islands lie between the latitude of 13° 16′ S and 14° 10′ S: their longitude, according to my reckoning, 15° 51′ to 17° 6′ W from the island Tofoa (by making a proportional allowance for the error afterwards found in the dead reckoning, I estimate the longitude of these islands to be from 167° 17′ E to 168° 34′ E from Greenwich). The largest island may be 20 leagues in circuit, the others 5 or 6. The easternmost is the smallest island, and most remarkable, having a high sugar-loaf hill.

The sight of these islands served but to increase the misery of our situation. We were very little better than starving, with plenty in view; yet to attempt procuring any relief was attended with so much danger, that prolonging of life, even in the midst of misery, was thought preferable, while there remained hopes of being able to surmount our hardships. For my own part, I consider the general run of cloudy and wet weather to be a blessing of Providence. Hot weather would have caused us to have died with thirst; and perhaps being so constantly covered with rain or sea protected us from that dreadful calamity.

As I had nothing to assist my memory I could not determine whether these islands were a part of the New Hebrides or not: I believed them perfectly a new discovery, which I have since found to be the case; but, though they were not seen either by Monsieur Bougainville or Captain Cook, they are so nearly in the neighbourhood of the New Hebrides, that they must be considered as part of the same group. They are fertile, and inhabited, as I saw smoke in several places.

Saturday 16th May

Fresh gales from the SE, and rainy weather. The night was very dark, not a star to be seen to steer by, and the sea breaking constantly over us. I found it necessary to act as much as possible against the southerly winds, to prevent being driven too near New Guinea; for in general we were forced to keep so much before the sea, that if we had not, at intervals of moderate weather, steered a more southerly course, we should inevitably, from a continuance of the gales, have been thrown in sight of that coast: in which case there would most probably have been an end to our voyage.

In addition to our miserable allowance of one 25th of a pound of bread, and a quarter of a pint of water, I issued for dinner about an ounce of salt pork to each person. I was often solicited for this pork, but I considered it better to give it in small quantities than to use all at once or twice, which would have been done if I had allowed it.

At noon I observed, in 13° 33´ S; longitude made from Tofoa, 19° 27´ W; course N 82° W; distance 101 miles. The sun gave us hopes of drying our wet clothes.

Sunday 17th May

The sunshine was but of short duration. We had strong breezes at SE by S, and dark gloomy weather, with storms of thunder, lightning, and rain. The night was truly horrible, and not a star to be seen; so that our steerage was uncertain. At dawn of day I found every person complaining, and some of them soliciting extra allowance; but I positively refused it. Our situation was extremely miserable; always wet, and suffering extreme cold in the night, without the least shelter from the weather. Being constantly obliged to bail, to keep the boat from filling, was, perhaps, not to be reckoned an evil, as it gave us exercise.

The little rum I had was of great service to us; when our nights were particularly distressing, I generally served a teaspoonful or two to each person: and it was always joyful tidings when they heard of my intentions.

At noon a waterspout was very near on board of us. I issued an ounce of pork, in addition to the allowance of bread and water; but before we began to eat, every person stript and wrung their clothes through the sea-water, which we found warm and refreshing. Course since yesterday noon WSW; distance 100 miles; latitude, by account, 14° 11´ S, and longitude made 21° 3´ W.

Monday 18th May

Fresh gales with rain, and a dark dismal night, wind SE; the sea constantly breaking over us, and nothing but the wind and sea to direct our steerage. I now fully determined to make New Holland, to the southward of Endeavour straits, sensible that it was necessary to preserve such a situation as would make a southerly wind a fair one; that I might range the reefs until an opening should be found into smooth water, and we the sooner be able to pick up some refreshments.

In the morning the rain abated, when we stripped, and wrung our clothes through the sea-water, as usual, which refreshed us wonderfully. Every person complained of violent pain in their bones: I was only surprised that no one was yet laid up. Served one 25th of a pound of bread, and a quarter of a pint of water, at supper, breakfast, and dinner, as customary.

At noon I deduced my situation, by account, for we had no glimpse of the sun, to be in latitude 14° 52′ S; course since yesterday noon WSW 106 miles; longitude made from Tofoa 22° 45′ W. Saw many boobies and noddies, a sign of being in the neighbourhood of land.

Tuesday 19th May

Fresh gales at ENE, with heavy rain, and dark gloomy weather, and no sight of the sun. We passed this day miserably wet and cold, covered with rain and sea, from which we had no relief, but at intervals by pulling off our clothes and wringing them through the sea-water. In the night we had very severe lightning, but otherwise it was so dark that we could not see each other. The morning produced many complaints on the severity of the weather, and I would gladly have issued my allowance of rum, if it had not appeared to me that we were to suffer much more, and that it was necessary to preserve the little I had, to give relief at a time we might be less able to bear such hardships; but, to make up for it, I served out about half an ounce of pork to each person, with the common allowance of bread and water, for dinner. All night and day we were obliged to bail without intermission.

At noon it was very bad weather and constant rain; latitude, by account, 14° 37′ S; course since yesterday N 81° W; distance 100 miles; longitude made 24° 30′ W.

Wednesday 20th May

Fresh breezes ENE with constant rain; at times a deluge. Always bailing.

At dawn of day, some of my people seemed half dead: our appearances were horrible; and I could look no way, but I caught the eye of someone in distress. Extreme hunger was now too evident, but no one suffered from thirst, nor had we much inclination to drink, that desire, perhaps, being satisfied through the skin. The little sleep we got was in the midst of water, and we constantly awoke with severe cramps and pains in our bones. This morning I served about two teaspoonfuls of rum to each person, and the allowance of bread and water, as usual. At noon the sun broke out, and revived everyone. I found we were in latitude 14° 49′ S; longitude made 25° 46′ W; course S 88° W; distance 75 miles.

Thursday 21st May

Fresh gales, and heavy showers of rain. Wind ENE.

Our distresses were now very great, and we were so covered with rain and salt water, that we could scarcely see. Sleep, though we longed for it, afforded no comfort: for my own part, I almost lived without it: we suffered extreme cold, and everyone dreaded the approach of night. About 2 o'clock in the morning we were overwhelmed with a deluge of rain. It fell so heavy that we were afraid it would fill the boat, and were obliged to bail with all our might. At dawn of day, I served a large allowance of rum. Towards noon the rain abated and the sun shone, but we were miserably cold and wet, the sea breaking so constantly over us, that, notwithstanding the heavy rain, we had not been able to add to our stock of fresh water. The usual allowance of one 25th of a pound of bread and water was served at evening, morning, and noon. Latitude, by observation, 14° 29′ S, and longitude made, by account, from Tofoa, 27° 25′ W; course, since yesterday noon, N 78° W, 99 miles. I now considered myself on a meridian with the east part of New Guinea, and about 65 leagues distant from the coast of New Holland.

Friday 22nd May
Strong gales from ESE to SSE, a high sea, and dark dismal night.

Our situation this day was extremely calamitous. We were obliged to take the course of the sea, running right before it, and watching with the utmost care, as the least error in the helm would in a moment have been our destruction. The sea was continually breaking all over us; but, as we suffered not such cold as when wet with the rain, I only served the common allowance of bread and water.

At noon it blew very hard, and the foam of the sea kept running over our stern and quarters; I however got propped up, and made an observation of the latitude, in 14° 17′ S; course N 85° W; distance 130 miles; longitude made 29° 38′ west.

Saturday 23rd May

Strong gales with very hard squalls, and rain; wind SE, and SSE.

The misery we suffered this day exceeded the preceding. The night was dreadful. The sea flew over us with great force, and kept us bailing with horror and anxiety. At dawn of day I found everyone in a most distressed condition, and I now began to fear that another such a night would put an end to the lives of several who seemed no longer able to support such sufferings. Everyone complained of severe pains in their bones; but these were alleviated, in some degree, by an allowance of two teaspoonfuls of rum; after drinking which, having wrung our clothes, and taken our breakfast of bread and water, we became a little refreshed.

Towards noon it became fair weather; but with very little abatement of the gale, and the sea remained equally high. With great difficulty I observed the latitude to be 13° 44′ S; course N 74° W; distance 116 miles since yesterday; longitude made 31° 32′ W from Tofoa.

Sunday 24th May

Fresh gales and fine weather; wind SSE and S.

Towards the evening the weather looked much better, which rejoiced all hands, so that they eat their scanty allowance with more satisfaction than for some time past. The night also was fair; but, being always wet with the sea, we suffered much from the cold. A fine morning, I had the pleasure to see, produced some cheerful countenances. Towards noon the weather improved, and, the first time for 15 days past, we found a little warmth from the sun. We stripped, and hung our clothes up to dry, which were by this time become so threadbare, that they would not keep out either wet or cold.

At noon I observed in latitude 13° 33´ S; longitude, by account, from Tofoa 33° 28´ W; course N 84° W; distance 114 miles. With the usual allowance of bread and water for dinner, I served an ounce of pork to each person.

Monday 25th May
Fresh gales and fair weather. Wind SSE.

This afternoon we had many birds about us, which are never seen far from land, such as boobies and noddies.

About 3 o'clock the sea began to run fair, and we shipped but little water, I therefore determined to know the exact quantity of bread I had left; and on examining found, according to my present issues, sufficient for 29 days allowance. In the course of this time I hoped to be at Timor; but, as that was very uncertain, and perhaps after all we might be obliged to go to Java, I determined to proportion my issues to six weeks. I was apprehensive that this would be ill received, and that it would require my utmost resolution to enforce it; for, small as the quantity was which I intended to take away, for our future good, yet it might appear to my people like robbing them of life, and some, who were less patient than their companions, I expected would very ill brook it. I however represented it so essentially necessary to guard against delays in our voyage by contrary winds, or other causes, promising to enlarge upon the allowance as we got on, that it was readily agreed to. I therefore fixed, that every person should receive one 25th of a pound of bread for breakfast, and one 25th of a pound for dinner; so that by omitting the proportion for supper, I had 43 days allowance.

At noon some noddies came so near to us that one of them was caught by hand. This bird is about the size of a small pigeon. I divided it, with its entrails, into 18 portions, and by the method of, 'Who shall have this?' (one person turns his back on the object that is to be divided: another then points separately to the portions, at each of them asking aloud, 'Who shall have this?' to which the first answers by naming somebody – this impartial method of division gives every man an equal chance of the best share) it was distributed with the allowance of bread and water for dinner, and eat up bones and all, with salt water for sauce. I observed the latitude 13° 32´ S; longitude made 35° 19´ W; and course N 89° W; distance 108 miles.

Tuesday 26th May
Fresh gales at SSE, and fine weather.

In the evening we saw several boobies flying so near to us that we caught one of them by hand. This bird is as large as a good duck; like the noddy, it has received its name from seamen, for suffering itself to be caught on the masts and yards of ships. They are the most presumptive proofs of being in the neighbourhood of land of any sea-fowl we are acquainted with. I directed the bird to be killed for supper, and the blood to be given to three of the people who were the most distressed for want of food. The body, with the entrails, beak, and feet, I divided into 18 shares, and with an allowance of bread, which I made a merit of granting, we made a good supper, compared with our usual fare.

In the morning we caught another booby, so that Providence seemed to be relieving our wants in a very extraordinary manner. Towards noon we passed a great many pieces of the branches of trees, some of which appeared to have been no long time in the water. I had a good observation for the latitude, and found my situation to be in 13° 41´ S; my longitude, by account, from Tofoa, 37° 13´ W; course S 85° W, 112 miles. Every person was now overjoyed at the addition to their dinner, which I distributed as I had done in the evening; giving the blood to those who were the most in want of food.

To make our bread a little savoury we frequently dipped it in salt water; but for my own part I generally broke mine into small pieces, and ate it in my allowance of water, out of a coconut shell, with a spoon, economically avoiding to take too large a piece at a time, so that I was as long at dinner as if it had been a much more plentiful meal.

Wednesday 27th May
Fresh breezes south-easterly, and fine weather.

The weather was now serene, but unhappily we found ourselves unable to bear the sun's heat; many of us suffering a languor and faintness, which made life indifferent. We were, however, so fortunate as to catch two boobies today; their stomachs contained several flying-fish and small cuttlefish, all of which I saved to be divided for dinner.

We passed much drift wood, and saw many birds; I therefore did not hesitate to pronounce that we were near the reefs of New Holland, and assured everyone I would make the coast without delay, in the parallel we were in, and range the reef till I found an opening, through which we might get into smooth water, and pick up some supplies. From my recollection of Captain Cook's survey of this coast, I considered the direction of it to be NW, and I was therefore satisfied that, with the wind to the southward of E, I could always clear any dangers.

At noon I observed in latitude 13° 26′ S; course since yesterday N 82° W; distance 109 miles; longitude made 39° 4′ W. After writing my account, I divided the two birds with their entrails, and the contents of their maws, into 18 portions, and, as the prize was a very valuable one, it was divided as before, by calling out 'Who shall have this?' so that today, with the allowance of a 25th of a pound of bread at breakfast, and another at dinner, with the proportion of water, I was happy to see that every person thought he had feasted.

Thursday 28th May
Fresh breezes and fair weather; wind ESE and E.

In the evening we saw a gannet; and the clouds remained so fixed in the west, that I had little doubt of our being near to New Holland; and every person, after taking his allowance of water for supper, began to divert himself with conversing on the probability of what we should find.

At one in the morning the person at the helm heard the sound of breakers, and I no sooner lifted up my head than I saw them close under our lee, not more than a quarter of a mile distant from us. I immediately hauled on a wind to the NNE, and in ten minutes time we could neither see nor hear them.

I have already mentioned my reason for making New Holland so far to the southward; for I never doubted of numerous openings in the reef, through which I could have access to the shore: and, knowing the inclination of the coast to be to the NW, and the wind mostly to the southward of E, I could with ease range such a barrier of reefs till I should find a passage, which now became absolutely necessary, without a moment's loss of time. The idea of getting into smooth water, and finding refreshments, kept my people's spirits up: their joy was very great after we had got clear of the breakers, to which we had been much nearer than I thought was possible to be before we saw them.

In the morning, at daylight, I bore away again for the reefs, and saw them by 9 o'clock. The sea broke furiously over every part, and I had no sooner got near to them than the wind came at E, so that we could only lie along the line of the breakers, within which we saw the water so smooth, that every person already anticipated the heartfelt satisfaction he would receive as soon as we could get within them. But I now found we were embayed, for I could not lie clear with my sails, the wind having backed against us, and the sea set in so heavy towards the reef that our situation was become dangerous. We could effect but little with the oars, having scarce strength to pull them; and it was becoming every minute more and more probable that we should be obliged to attempt pushing over the reef, in case we could not pull off. Even this I did not despair of effecting with success, when happily we discovered a break in the reef, about one mile from us, and at the same time an island of a moderate height within it, nearly in the same direction, bearing W 1/2 N. I entered the passage with a strong stream running to the westward; and found it about a quarter of a mile broad, with every appearance of deep water.

On the outside, the reef inclined to the NE for a few miles, and from thence to the NW; on the south side of the entrance, it inclined to the SSW as far as I could see it; and I conjecture that a similar passage to this which we now entered, may be found near the breakers that I first discovered, which are 23 miles S of this channel.

I did not recollect what latitude Providential Channel lies in but I considered it to be within a few miles of this, which is situate in 12° 51´ S latitude. (Providential Channel is in 12° 34´ S, longitude 143° 33´ E.)

Being now happily within the reefs, and in smooth water, I endeavoured to keep near them to try for fish; but the tide set us to the NW; I therefore bore away in that direction, and, having promised to land on the first convenient spot we could find, all our past hardships seemed already to be forgotten.

At noon I had a good observation, by which our latitude was 12° 46´ S, whence the foregoing situations may be considered as determined with some exactness. The island first seen bore WSW 5 leagues. This, which I have called the island Direction, will in fair weather always shew the channel, from which it bears due W, and may be seen as soon as the reefs, from a ship's mast-head: it lies in the latitude of 12° 51´ S. These, however, are marks too small for a ship to hit, unless it can hereafter be ascertained that passages through the reef are numerous along the coast, which I am inclined to think they are, and then there would be little risk if the wind was not directly on the shore.

My longitude, made by dead reckoning, from the island Tofoa to our passage through the reef, is 40° 10´ W. Providential channel, I imagine, must lie very nearly under the same meridian with our passage; by which it appears we had outrun our reckoning 1° 9´.

We now returned God thanks for His gracious protection, and with much content took our miserable allowance of a 25th of a pound of bread, and a quarter of a pint of water, for dinner.

Friday 29th May

Moderate breezes and fine weather, wind ESE.

As we advanced within the reefs, the coast began to shew itself very distinctly, with a variety of high and low land; some parts of which were covered with wood. In our way towards the shore we fell in with a point of a reef, which is connected with that towards the sea, and here I came to a grapnel, and tried to catch fish, but had no success. The island Direction now bore S 3 or 4 leagues. Two islands lay about four miles to the W by N, and appeared eligible for a resting-place, if nothing more; but on my approach to the first I found it only a heap of stones, and its size too inconsiderable to shelter the boat. I therefore proceeded to the next, which was close to it and towards the main, where, on the NW side, I found a bay and a fine sandy point to land at. Our distance was about a quarter of a mile from a projecting part of the main, bearing from SW by S, to NNW 3/4 W. I now landed to examine if there were any signs of the natives being near us; but though I discovered some old fire-places, I saw nothing to alarm me for our situation during the night. Everyone was anxious to find something to eat, and I soon heard that there were oysters on the rocks, for the tide was out; but it was nearly dark, and only a few could be gathered. I determined therefore to wait till the morning, to know how to proceed, and I consented that one half of us should sleep on shore, and the other in the boat. We would gladly have made a fire but, as we could not accomplish it, we took our rest for the night, which happily was calm and undisturbed.

The dawn of day brought greater strength and spirits to us than I expected; for, notwithstanding everyone was very weak, there appeared strength sufficient remaining to make me conceive the most favourable hopes of our being able to surmount the difficulties we might yet have to encounter.

As soon as I saw that there were not any natives immediately near us, I sent out parties in search of supplies, while others were putting the boat in order, that I might be ready to go to sea in case any unforeseen cause might make it necessary. The first object of this work that demanded our attention was the rudder: one of the gudgeons had come out, in the course of the night, and was lost. This, if it had happened at sea, would probably have been the cause of our perishing, as the management of the boat could not have been so nicely preserved as these very heavy seas required. I had often expressed my fears of this accident, and, that we might be prepared for it, had taken the precaution to have grummets fixed on each quarter of the boat for oars; but even our utmost readiness in using them, I fear, would not have saved us. It appears, therefore, a providential circumstance that it happened at this place, and was in our power to remedy the defect; for by great good luck we found a large staple in the boat that answered the purpose.

The parties were now returned, highly rejoiced at having found plenty of oysters and fresh water. I also had made a fire, by help of a small magnifying glass, that I always carried about me, to read off the divisions of my sextants; and, what was still more fortunate, among the few things which had been thrown into the boat and saved, was a piece of brimstone and a tinder-box, so that I secured fire for the future.

One of my people had been so provident as to bring away with him a copper pot: it was by being in possession of this article that I was enabled to make a proper use of the supply we found, for, with a mixture of bread and a little pork, I made a stew that might have been relished by people of more delicate appetites, of which each person received a full pint.

The general complaints of disease among us were a dizziness in the head, great weakness of the joints, and violent tenesmus, most of us having had no evacuation by stool since we left the ship. I had constantly a severe pain at my stomach; but none of our complaints were alarming; on the contrary, everyone retained marks of strength, that, with a mind possessed of any fortitude, could bear more fatigue than I hoped we had to undergo in our voyage to Timor.

As I would not allow the people to expose themselves to the heat of the sun, it being near noon, everyone took his allotment of earth, shaded by the bushes, for a short sleep.

The oysters we found grew so fast to the rocks that it was with difficulty they could be broke off, and at last we discovered it to be the most expeditious way to open them where they were found. They were very sizeable, and well tasted, and gave us great relief. To add to this happy circumstance, in the hollow of the land there grew some wire grass, which indicated a moist situation. On forcing a stick, about three feet long, into the ground, we found water, and with little trouble dug a well, which produced as much as we were in need of. It was very good, but I could not determine if it was a spring or not. Our wants made it not necessary to make the well deep, for it flowed as fast as we emptied it; which, as the soil was apparently too loose to retain water from the rains, renders it probable to be a spring. It lies about 200 yards to the SE of a point in the SW part of the island.

I found evident signs of the natives resorting to this island; for, besides fire-places, I saw two miserable wigwams, having only one side loosely covered. We found a pointed stick, about three feet long, with a slit in the end of it, to sling stones with, the same as the natives of Van Diemen's land use.

The track of some animal was very discernible, and Mr Nelson agreed with me that it was the kangaroo; but how these animals can get from the main I know not, unless brought over by the natives to breed, that they may take them with more ease, and render a supply of food certain to them; as on the continent the catching of them may be precarious, or attended with great trouble, in so large an extent of country.

The island may be about two miles in circuit; it is a high lump of rocks and stones covered with wood; but the trees are small, the soil, which is very indifferent and sandy, being barely sufficient to produce them. The trees that came within our knowledge were the manchineal and a species of purow: also some palm-trees, the tops of which we cut down, and the soft interior part or heart of them was so palatable that it made a good addition to our mess. Mr Nelson discovered some fern-roots, which I thought might be good roasted, as a substitute for bread, but it proved a very poor one: it however was very good in its natural state to allay thirst, and on that account I directed a quantity to be collected to take into the boat. Many pieces of coconut shells and husk were found about the shore, but we could find no coconut trees, neither did I see any like them on the main.

I had cautioned everyone not to touch any kind of berry or fruit that they might find; yet they were no sooner out of my sight than they began to make free with three different kinds that grew all over the island, eating without any reserve. The symptoms of having eaten too much began at last to frighten same of them; but on questioning others, who had taken a more moderate allowance, their minds were a little quieted. The others, however, became equally alarmed in their turn, dreading that such symptoms would come on, and that they were all poisoned, so that they regarded each other with the strongest marks of apprehension, uncertain what would be the issue of their imprudence. Happily the fruit proved wholesome and good. One sort grew on a small delicate kind of vine; they were the size of a large gooseberry, and very like in substance, but had only a sweet taste; the skin was a pale red, streaked with yellow the long way of the fruit: it was pleasant and agreeable. Another kind grew on bushes, like that which is called the sea-side grape in the West Indies; but the fruit was very different, and more like elder-berries, growing in clusters in the same manner. The third sort was a black berry, not in such plenty as the others, and resembled a bullace, or large kind of sloe, both in size and taste. Seeing these fruits eaten by the birds made me consider them fit for use, and those who had already tried the experiment, not finding any bad effect, made it a certainty that we might eat of them without danger.

Wild pigeons, parrots, and other birds, were about the summit of the island, but, as I had no firearms, relief of that kind was not to be expected, unless I met with some unfrequented spot where we might take them with our hands.

On the south side of the island, and about half a mile from the well, a small run of water was found; but, as its source was not traced, I know nothing more of it.

The shore of this island is very rocky, except the part we landed at, and here I picked up many pieces of pumice-stone. On the part of the main next to us were several sandy bays, but at low-water they became an extensive rocky flat. The country had rather a barren appearance, except in a few places where it was covered with wood. A remarkable range of rocks lay a few miles to the SW, or a high peaked hill terminated the coast towards the sea, with other high lands and islands to the southward. A high fair cape showed the direction of the coast to the NW, about 7 leagues, and two small isles lay 3 or 4 leagues to the northward.

I saw a few bees or wasps, several lizards, and the blackberry bushes were full of ants nests, webbed as a spider's, but so close and compact as not to admit the rain.

A trunk of a tree, about 50 feet long, lay on the beach; from whence I conclude a heavy sea runs in here with the northerly winds.

This being the day of the restoration of King Charles the Second, and the name not being inapplicable to our present situation (for we were restored to fresh life and strength), I named this Restoration Island; for I thought it probable that Captain Cook might not have taken notice of it. The other names I have presumed to give the different parts of the coast will be only to show my route a little more distinctly.

At noon I found the latitude of the island to be 12° 39´ S; our course having been N 66° W; distance 18 miles from yesterday noon.

Saturday 30th May
Very fine weather, and ESE winds. This afternoon I sent parties out again to gather oysters, with which and some of the inner part of the palm-top, we made another good stew for supper, each person receiving a full pint and a half; but I refused bread to this meal, for I considered our wants might yet be very great, and as such I represented the necessity of saving our principal support whenever it was in our power.

At night we again divided, and one half of us slept on shore by a good fire. In the morning I discovered a visible alteration in every one for the better, and I sent them away again to gather oysters. I had now only 2 lb of pork left. This article, which I could not keep under lock and key as I did the bread, had been pilfered by some inconsiderate person, but everyone most solemnly denied it; I therefore resolved to put it out of their power for the future, by sharing what remained for our dinner. While the party was out getting oysters I got the boat in readiness for sea and filled all our water vessels, which amounted to nearly 60 gallons.

The party being returned, dinner was soon ready, and everyone had as good an allowance as they had for supper; for with the pork I gave an allowance of bread; as I was determined forthwith to push on. As it was not yet noon, I told every one that an exertion should be made to gather as many oysters as possible for a sea store, as I was determined to sail in the afternoon.

At noon I again observed the latitude 12° 39´ S; it was then high-water, the tide had risen three feet, but I could not be certain which way the flood came from. I deduce the time of high-water at full and change to be ten minutes past seven in the morning.

Sunday 31st May

Early in the afternoon, the people returned with the few oysters they had time to pick up, and everything was put into the boat. I then examined the quantity of bread remaining, and found 38 days allowance, according to the last mode of issuing a 25th of a pound at breakfast and at dinner.

Fair weather, and moderate breezes at ESE and SE.

Being all ready for sea, I directed every person to attend prayers, and by 4 o'clock we were preparing to embark; when twenty natives appeared, running and holloaing to us, on the opposite shore. They were armed with a spear or lance, and a short weapon which they carried in their left hand: they made signs for us to come to them. On the top of the hills we saw the heads of many more; whether these were their wives and children, or others who waited for our landing, until which they meant not to show themselves, lest we might be intimidated, I cannot say; but, as I found we were discovered to be on the coast, I thought it prudent to make the best of my way, for fear of canoes; though, from the accounts of Captain Cook, the chance was that there were very few or none of any consequence. I passed these people as near as I could, which was within a quarter of a mile; they were naked, and apparently black, and their hair or wool bushy and short.

I directed my course within two small islands that lie to the north of Restoration Island, passing between them and the main land, towards Fair Cape, with a strong tide in my favour; so that I was abreast of it by 8 o'clock. The coast I had passed was high and woody. As I could see no land without Fair Cape, I concluded that the coast inclined to the NW and WNW, which was agreeable to my recollection of Captain Cook's survey. I therefore steered more towards the W; but by 11 o'clock at night I found myself mistaken: for we met with low land, which inclined to the NE; so that at 3 o'clock in the morning I found we were embayed, which obliged us to stand back to the southward.

At daybreak I was exceedingly surprised to find the appearance of the country all changed, as if in the course of the night I had been transported to another part of the world; for we had now a miserable low sandy coast in view, with very little verdure, or anything to indicate that it was at all habitable to a human being, if I except some patches of small trees or brush-wood.

I had many small islands in view to the NE, about six miles distant. The E part of the main bore N four miles, and Fair Cape SSE 5 or 6 leagues. I took the channel between the nearest island and the main land, about one mile apart, leaving all the islands on the starboard side. Some of these were very pretty spots, covered with wood, and well situated for fishing; large shoals of fish were about us, but we could not catch any. As I was passing this strait we saw another party of Indians, seven in number, running towards us, shouting and making signs for us to land. Some of them waved green branches of the bushes which were near them, as a sign of friendship; but there were some of their other motions less friendly. A larger party we saw a little farther off, and coming towards us. I therefore determined not to land, though I wished much to have had some intercourse with these people; for which purpose I beckoned to them to come near to me, and laid the boat close to the rocks; but not one would come within 200 yards of us. They were armed in the same manner as those I had seen from Restoration Island, were stark naked, and appeared to be jet black, with short bushy hair or wool, and in every respect the same people. An island of good height now bore N 1/2 W, four miles from us, at which I resolved to see what could be got, and from thence to take a look at the coast. At this isle I landed about 8 o'clock in the morning. The shore was rocky, with some sandy beaches within the rocks: the water, however, was smooth, and I landed without difficulty. I sent two parties out, one to the northward, and the other to the southward, to seek for supplies, and others I ordered to stay by the boat. On this occasion their fatigue and weakness so far got the better of their sense of duty, that some of them began to mutter who had done most, and declared they would rather be without their dinner than go in search of it. One person, in particular, went so far as to tell me, with a mutinous look, he was as good a man as myself. It was not possible for me to judge where this might have an end, if not stopped in time; I therefore determined to strike a final blow at it, and either to preserve my command, or die in the attempt: and, seizing a cutlass, I ordered him to take hold of another and defend himself; on which he called out I was going to kill him, and began to make concessions. I did not allow this to interfere further with the harmony of the boat's crew, and everything soon became quiet.

The parties continued collecting what could be found, which consisted of some fine oysters and clams, and a few small dog-fish that were caught in the holes of the rocks. We also found about two tons of rainwater in the hollow of the rocks, on the north part of the island, so that of this essential article we were again so happy as not to be in want.

After regulating the mode of proceeding, I set off for the highest part of the island, to see and consider of my route for the night. To my surprise I could see no more of the main than I did from below, it extending only from S 1/2 E, four miles, to W by N, about 3 leagues, full of sand-hills. Besides the isles to the ESE and south, that I had seen before, I could only discover a small key NW by N. As this was considerably farther from the main than where I was at present, I resolved to get there by night, it being a more secure resting-place; for I was here open to an attack, if the Indians had canoes, as they undoubtedly observed my landing. My mind being made up on this point, I returned, taking a particular look at the spot I was on, which I found only to produce a few bushes and coarse grass, and the extent of the whole not two miles in circuit. On the north side, in a sandy bay, I saw an old canoe, about 33 feet long, lying bottom upwards, and half buried in the beach. It was made of three pieces, the bottom entire, to which the sides were sewed in the common way. It had a sharp projecting prow rudely carved, in resemblance of the head of a fish; the extreme breadth was about three feet, and I imagine it was capable of carrying 20 men.

At noon the parties were all returned, but had found difficulty in gathering the oysters, from their close adherence to the rocks, and the clams were scarce: I therefore saw, that it would be of little use to remain longer in this place, as we should not be able to collect more than we could eat; nor could any tolerable sea-store be expected, unless we fell in with a greater plenty. I named this Sunday Island: it lies N by W 3/4 W from Restoration Island; the latitude, by a good observation, 11° 58´ S.

Monday 1st June
Fresh breezes and fair weather, ending with a fresh gale. Wind SE by S.

At 2 o'clock in the afternoon we dined; each person having a full pint and a half of stewed oysters and clams, thickened with small beans, which Mr Nelson informed us were a species of dolichos. Having eaten heartily, and taken the water we were in want of, I only waited to determine the time of high-water, which I found to be at 3 o'clock, and the rise of the tide about five feet. According to this it is high-water on the full and change at 19 minutes past 9 in the morning; but here I observed the flood to come from the southward, though at Restoration Island, I thought it came from the northward. I think Captain Cook mentions that he found great irregularity in the set of the flood on this coast.

I now sailed for the key which I had seen in the NW by N, giving the name of Sunday Island to the place I left; we arrived just at dark, but found it so surrounded by a reef of rocks, that I could not land without danger of staving the boat; and on that account I came to a grapnel for the night.

At dawn of day we got on shore, and tracked the boat into shelter; for the wind blowing fresh without, and the ground being rocky, I was afraid to trust her at a grapnel, lest she might be blown to sea: I was, therefore, obliged to let her ground in the course of the ebb. From appearances, I expected that if we remained till night we should meet with turtle, as we had already discovered recent tracks of them. Innumerable birds of the noddy kind made this island their resting-place; so that I had reason to flatter myself with hopes of getting supplies in greater abundance than it had hitherto been in my power. The situation was at least 4 leagues distant from the main. We were on the north-westernmost of four small keys, which were surrounded by a reef of rocks connected by sand-banks, except between the two northernmost; and there likewise it was dry at low water; the whole forming a lagoon island, into which the tide flowed: at this entrance I kept the boat.

As usual, I sent parties away in search of supplies, but, to our great disappointment, we could only get a few clams and some dolichos: with these, and the oysters we had brought from Sunday Island, I made up a mess for dinner, with an addition of a small quantity of bread.

Towards noon, Mr Nelson and his party, who had been to the easternmost key, returned; but himself in such a weak condition, that he was obliged to be supported by two men. His complaint was a violent heat in his bowels, a loss of sight, much drought, and an inability to walk. This I found was occasioned by his being unable to support the heat of the sun, and that, when he was fatigued and faint, instead of retiring into the shade to rest, he had continued to do more than his strength was equal to. It was a great satisfaction to me to find that he had no fever; and it was now that the little wine, which I had so carefully saved, became of real use. I gave it in very small quantities, with some small pieces of bread soaked in it; and, having pulled off his clothes, and laid him under some shady bushes, he began to recover. The boatswain and carpenter also were ill, and complained of headache, and sickness of the stomach; others, who had not had any evacuation by stool, became shockingly distressed with the tenesmus; so that there were but few without complaints. An idea now prevailed, that their illness was occasioned by eating the dolichos, and some were so much alarmed that they thought themselves poisoned. Myself, however, and some others, who had eaten of them, were yet very well; but the truth was, that all those who were complaining, except Mr Nelson, had gorged themselves with a large quantity of raw beans, and Mr Nelson informed me, that they were constantly teasing him, whenever a berry was found, to know if it was good to eat; so that it would not have been surprising if many of them had been really poisoned.

Our dinner was not so well relished as at Sunday Island, because we had mixed the dolichos with our stew. The oysters and soup, however, were eaten by everyone except Mr Nelson, whom I fed with a few small pieces of bread soaked in half a glass of wine, and he continued to mend.

In my walk round the island, I found several coconut shells, the remains of an old wigwam, and the backs of two turtle, but no sign of any quadruped. One of my people found three sea-fowl's eggs.

As is common on such spots, the soil is little other than sand, yet it produced small toa-trees, and some others, that we were not acquainted with. There were fish in the lagoon, but we could not catch any. As our wants, therefore, were not likely to be supplied here, not even with water for our daily expence, I determined to sail in the morning, after trying our success in the night for turtle and birds. A quiet night's rest also, I conceived, would be of essential service to those who were unwell.

From the wigwam and turtle-shell being found, it is certain that the natives sometimes resort to this place, and have canoes: but I did not apprehend that we ran any risk by remaining here. I directed our fire, however, to be made in the thicket, that we might not be discovered in the night.

At noon, I observed the latitude of this island to be 11° 47′ S. The main land extended towards the NW, and was full of white sand-hills: another small island lay within us, bearing W by N 1/4 N, 3 leagues distant. My situation being very low, I could see nothing of the reef towards the sea.

Tuesday 2nd June

The first part of this day we had some light showers of rain; the latter part was fair, wind from the SE, blowing fresh.

Rest was now so much wanted that the afternoon was advantageously spent in sleep. There were, however, a few not disposed to it, and those I employed in dressing some clams to take with us for the next day's dinner; others we cut up in slices to dry, which I knew was the most valuable supply we could find here. But, contrary to our expectation, they were very scarce.

Towards evening, I cautioned everyone against making too large a fire, or suffering it after dark to blaze up. Mr Samuel and Mr Peckover had the superintendence of this business, while I was strolling about the beach to observe if I thought it could be seen from the main. I was just satisfied that it could not, when on a sudden the island appeared all in a blaze, that might have been seen at a much more considerable distance. I ran to learn the cause, and found it was occasioned by the imprudence and obstinacy of one of the party, who, in my absence, had insisted on having a fire to himself; in making which the flames caught the neighbouring grass and rapidly spread. This misconduct might have produced very serious consequences, by discovering our situation to the natives; for, if they had attacked us, we must inevitably have fallen a sacrifice, as we had neither arms nor strength to oppose an enemy. Thus the relief which I expected from a little sleep was totally lost, and I anxiously waited for the flowing of the tide, that we might proceed to sea.

I found it high-water at half past five this evening, whence I deduce the time, on the full and change of the moon, to be 58' past 10 in the morning: the rise is nearly five feet. I could not observe the set of the flood; but imagine it comes from the southward, and that I have been mistaken at Restoration Island, as I find the time of high-water gradually later as we advance to the northward.

After 8 o'clock, Mr Samuel and Mr Peckover went out to watch for turtle, and three men went to the east key to endeavour to catch birds. All the others complaining of being sick took their rest, except Mr Hayward and Mr Elphinston, who I directed to keep watch. About midnight the bird party returned with only twelve noddies, a bird I have already described to be about the size of a pigeon: but if it had not been for the folly and obstinacy of one of the party, who separated from the other two, and disturbed the birds, they might have caught a great number. I was so much provoked at my plans being thus defeated that I gave the offender (Robert Lamb – this man, when he came to Java, acknowledged he had eaten nine birds on the key, after he separated from the other two) a good beating. I now went in search of the turtling party, who had taken great pains, but without success. This, however, did not surprise me, as it was not to be expected that turtle would come near us after the noise which was made at the beginning of the evening in extinguishing the fire. I therefore desired them to come back, but they requested to stay a little longer, as they still hoped to find some before daylight: they, however, returned by 3 o'clock, without any reward for their labour.

The birds we half dressed, which, with a few clams, made the whole of the supply procured here. I tied up a few gilt buttons and some pieces of iron to a tree, for any of the natives that might come after us; and, happily finding my invalids much better for their night's rest, I got everyone into the boat, and departed by dawn of day. Wind at SE; course to the N by W.

We had scarcely ran 2 leagues to the northward when the sea suddenly became rough, which not having experienced since we were within the reefs, I concluded to be occasioned by an open channel to the ocean. Soon afterwards we met with a large shoal, on which were two sandy keys; between these and two others, four miles to the west, I passed on to the northward, the sea still continuing to be rough.

Towards noon, I fell in with six other keys, most of which produced some small trees and brush-wood. These formed a pleasing contrast with the mainland we had passed, which was full of sand-hills. The country continued hilly, and the northernmost land, the same which we saw from the lagoon island, appeared like downs, sloping towards the sea. To the southward of this is a flat-topped hill, which, on account of its shape, I called Pudding-pan Hill, and a little to the northward two other hills, which we called the Paps; and here was a small tract of country without sand, the eastern part of which forms a cape, whence the coast inclines to the NW by N.

At noon I observed in the latitude of 11° 18′ S, the cape bearing W, distant ten miles. Five small keys bore from NE to SE, the nearest of them about two miles distant, and a low sandy key between us and the cape bore W, distant four miles. My course from the Lagoon Island N 1/2 W, distant 30 miles.

I am sorry it was not in my power to obtain a sufficient knowledge of the depth of water; for in our situation nothing could be undertaken that might have occasioned delay. It may however be understood, that, to the best of my judgment, from appearances, a ship may pass wherever I have omitted to represent danger.

I divided six birds, and issued one 25th of a pound of bread, with half a pint of water, to each person for dinner, and I gave half a glass of wine to Mr Nelson, who was now so far recovered as to require no other indulgence.

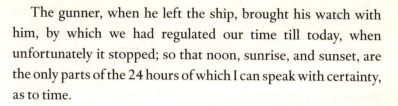

The gunner, when he left the ship, brought his watch with him, by which we had regulated our time till today, when unfortunately it stopped; so that noon, sunrise, and sunset, are the only parts of the 24 hours of which I can speak with certainty, as to time.

Wednesday 3rd June

Fresh gales SSE and SE, and fair weather. As we stood to the N by W this afternoon, we found more sea, which I attributed to our receiving less shelter from the reefs to the eastward: it is probable they do not extend so far to the N as this; at least, it may be concluded that there is not a continued barrier to prevent shipping having access to the shore. I observed that the stream set to the NW, which I considered to be the flood; in some places along the coast, we saw patches of wood.

At 5 o'clock, steering to the NW, we passed a large and fair inlet, into which, I imagine, is a safe and commodious entrance; it lies in latitude 11° S: about 3 leagues to the northward of this is an island, at which we arrived about sunset, and took shelter for the night under a sandy point, which was the only part we could land at: I was therefore under the necessity to put up with rather a wild situation, and slept in the boat. Nevertheless I sent a party away to see what could be got, but they returned without any success. They saw a great number of turtle bones and shells, where the natives had been feasting, and their last visit seemed to be of late date. The island was covered with wood, but in other respects a lump of rocks. We lay at a grapnel until daylight, with a very fresh gale and cloudy weather. The main bore from SE by S to NNW 1/2 W, 3 leagues; and a mountainous island, with a flat top, N by W, 4 or 5 leagues: several others were between it and the main. The spot we were on, which I call Turtle Island; lies in latitude, by account, 10° 52′ S, and 42 miles W from Restoration Island. Abreast of it the coast has the appearance of a sandy desert, but improves about 3 leagues farther to the northward, where it terminates in a point, near to which is a number of small islands. I sailed between these islands, where I found no bottom at twelve fathoms; the high mountainous island with a flat top, and four rocks to the SE of it, that I call the Brothers, being on my starboard hand. Soon after, an extensive opening appeared in the main land, with a number of high islands in it. I called this the Bay of Islands. We continued steering to the NW. Several islands and keys lay to the northward. The most northerly island was mountainous, having on it a very high round hill; and a smaller was remarkable for a single peaked hill.

The coast to the northward and westward of the Bay of Islands had a very different appearance from that to the southward. It was high and woody, with many islands close to it, and had a very broken appearance. Among these islands are fine bays, and convenient places for shipping. The northernmost I call Wednesday Island: to the NW of this we fell in with a large reef, which I believe joins a number of keys that were in sight from the NW to the ENE. We now stood to the SW half a league, when it was noon, and I had a good observation of the latitude in 10° 31′ S. Wednesday Island bore E by S five miles; the westernmost land SW 2 or 3 leagues; the islands to the northward, from NW by W 4 or 5 leagues, to NE 6 leagues; and the reef from W to NE, distant one mile, I now assured everyone that we should be clear of New Holland in the afternoon.

It is impossible for me to say how far this reef may extend. It may be a continuation, or a detached part of the range of shoals that surround the coast: but be that as it may, I consider the mountainous islands as separate from the shoals; and have no doubt that near them may be found good passages for ships. But I rather recommend to those who are to pass this strait from the eastward, to take their direction from the coast of New Guinea: yet, I likewise think that a ship coming from the southward will find a fair strait in the latitude of 10° S. I much wished to have ascertained this point; but in our distressful situation, any increase of fatigue, or loss of time, might have been attended with the most fatal consequences. I therefore determined to pass on without delay.

As an addition to our dinner of bread and water, I served to each person six oysters.

Thursday 4th June

A fresh gale at SE, and fair weather.

At 2 o'clock as we were steering to the SW, towards the westernmost part of the land in sight, we fell in with some large sand-banks that run off from the coast. We were therefore obliged to steer to the northward again, and, having got round them, I directed my course to the W.

At 4 o'clock, the westernmost of the islands to the northward bore N 4 leagues; Wednesday island E by N 5 leagues; and Shoal Cape SE by E 2 leagues. A small island was now seen bearing W, at which I arrived before dark, and found that it was only a rock, where boobies resort, for which reason I called it Booby Island. A small key also lies close to the W part of the coast, which I have called Shoal Cape. Here terminated the rocks and shoals of the

N part of New Holland, for, except Booby Island, we could see no land to the westward of S, after 3 o'clock this afternoon.

I find that Booby Island was seen by Captain Cook, and, by a remarkable coincidence of ideas, received from him the same name; but I cannot with certainty reconcile the situation of many parts of the coast that I have seen, to his survey. I ascribe this to the very different form in which land appears, when seen from the unequal heights of a ship and a boat. The chart I have given, is by no means meant to supersede that made by Captain Cook, who had better opportunities than I had, and was in every respect properly provided for surveying. The intention of mine is chiefly to render the narrative more intelligible, and to shew in what manner the coast appeared to me from an open boat. I have little doubt that the opening, which I named the Bay of Islands, is Endeavour Straits; and that our track was to the northward of Prince of Wales's Isles. Perhaps, by those who shall hereafter navigate these seas, more advantage may be derived from the possession of both our charts, than from either singly.

At 8 o'clock in the evening, we once more launched into the open ocean. Miserable as our situation was in every respect, I was secretly surprised to see that it did not appear to affect anyone so strongly as myself; on the contrary, it seemed as if they had embarked on a voyage to Timor, in a vessel sufficiently calculated for safety and convenience. So much confidence gave me great pleasure, and I may assert that to this cause their preservation is chiefly to be attributed; for if any one of them had despaired, he would most probably have died before we reached New Holland.

I now gave everyone hopes that eight or ten days might bring us to a land of safety; and, after praying to God for a continuance of his most gracious protection, I served an allowance of water for supper, and kept my course to the WSW, to counteract the southerly winds, in case they should blow strong.

We had been just six days on the coast of New Holland, in the course of which we found oysters, a few clams, some birds, and water. But perhaps a benefit nearly equal to this we received from not having fatigue in the boat, and enjoying good rest at night. These advantages certainly preserved our lives; for, small as the supply was, I am very sensible how much it relieved our distresses. About this time nature would have sunk under the extremes of hunger and fatigue. Some would have ceased to struggle for a life that only promised wretchedness and misery; while others, though possessed of more bodily strength, must soon have followed their unfortunate companions. Even in our present situation, we were most wretched spectacles; yet our fortitude and spirit remained; everyone being encouraged by the hopes of a speedy termination to his misery.

For my own part, wonderful as it may appear, I felt neither extreme hunger nor thirst. My allowance contented me, knowing I could have no more.

I served one 25th of a pound of bread, and an allowance of water, for breakfast, and the same for dinner, with an addition of six oysters to each person. At noon, latitude observed 10° 48´ S; course since yesterday noon S 81 W; distance 111 miles; longitude, by account, from Shoal Cape 1° 45´ W.

Friday 5th June

Fair weather with some showers, and a strong trade wind at ESE.

This day we saw a number of water-snakes, that were ringed yellow and black, and towards noon we passed a great deal of rock-weed. Though the weather was fair, we were constantly shipping water, and two men always employed to bail the boat.

At noon I observed in latitude 10° 45′ S; our course since yesterday W 1/4 N, 108 miles; longitude made 3° 35′ W. Served one 25th of a pound of bread, and a quarter of a pint of water for breakfast; the same for dinner, with an addition of six oysters; for supper water only.

Saturday 6th June

Fair weather, with some showers, and a fresh gale at SE and ESE. Constantly shipping water and baling.

In the evening a few boobies came about us, one of which I caught with my hand. The blood was divided among three of the men who were weakest, but the bird I ordered to be kept for our dinner the next day. Served a quarter of a pint of water for supper, and to some, who were most in need, half a pint.

In the course of the night we suffered much cold and shiverings. At daylight, I found that some of the clams, which had been hung up to dry for sea-store, were stolen; but everyone most solemnly denied having any knowledge of it. This forenoon we saw a gannet, a sand-lark, and some water-snakes, which in general were from two to three feet long.

Served the usual allowance of bread and water for breakfast, and the same for dinner, with the bird, which I distributed in the usual way, of 'Who shall have this?' I determined to make Timor about the latitude of 9° 30′ S, or 10° S. At noon I observed the latitude to be 10° 19′ S; course N 77° W; distance 117 miles; longitude made from the Shoal Cape, the north part of New Holland, 5° 31′ W.

Sunday 7th June

Fresh gales and fair weather till eight in the evening. The remaining part of the 24 hours squally, with much wind at SSE and ESE, and a high sea, so that we were constantly wet and bailing.

In the afternoon, I took an opportunity of examining again into our store of bread, and found remaining 19 days allowance, at my former rate of serving one 25th of a pound three times a day: therefore, as I saw every prospect of a quick passage, I again ventured to grant an allowance for supper, agreeable to my promise at the time it was discontinued.

We passed the night miserably wet and cold, and in the morning I heard heavy complaints of our deplorable situation. The sea was high and breaking over us. I could only afford the allowance of bread and water for breakfast; but for dinner I gave out an ounce of dried clams to each person, which was all that remained.

At noon I altered the course to the WNW, to keep more from the sea while it blew so strong. Latitude observed 9° 31´ S; course N 57° W; distance 88 miles; longitude made 6° 46´ W.

Monday 8th June

Fresh gales and squally weather, with some showers of rain. Wind E and ESE.

This day the sea ran very high, and we were continually wet, suffering much cold in the night. I now remarked that Mr Ledward, the surgeon, and Lawrence Lebogue, an old hardy seaman, were giving way very fast. I could only assist them by a teaspoonful or two of wine, which I had carefully saved, expecting such a melancholy necessity. Among most of the others I observed more than a common inclination to sleep, which seemed to indicate that nature was almost exhausted.

Served the usual allowance of bread and water at supper, breakfast, and dinner. Saw several gannets.

At noon I observed in 8° 45´ S; course WNW 1/4 W, 106 miles; longitude made 8° 23´ W.

Tuesday 9th June

Wind SE. The weather being moderate, I steered W by S.

At four in the afternoon we caught a small dolphin, the first relief of the kind we obtained. I issued about two ounces to each person, including the offals, and saved the remainder for dinner the next day. Towards evening the wind freshened, and it blew strong all night, so that we shipped much water, and suffered greatly from the wet and cold. At daylight, as usual, I heard much complaining, which my own feelings convinced me was too well founded. I gave the surgeon and Lebogue a little wine, but I could give no farther relief, than assurances that a very few days longer, at our present fine rate of sailing, would bring us to Timor.

Gannets, boobies, men of war and tropic birds, were constantly about us. Served the usual allowance of bread and water, and at noon dined on the remains of the dolphin, which amounted to about an ounce per man. I observed the latitude to be 9° 9´ S; longitude made 10° 8´ W; course since yesterday noon S 76° W; distance 107 miles.

Wednesday 10th June

Wind ESE. Fresh gales and fair weather, but a continuance of much sea, which, by breaking almost constantly over the boat, made us miserably wet, and we had much cold to endure in the night.

This afternoon I suffered great sickness from the oily nature of part of the stomach of the fish, which had fallen to my share at dinner. At sunset I served an allowance of bread and water for supper. In the morning, after a very bad night, I could see an alteration for the worse in more than half my people. The usual allowance was served for breakfast and dinner. At noon I found our situation to be in latitude 9° 16´ S; longitude from the north part of New Holland 12° 1´ W; course since yesterday noon W 1/2 S, distance 111 miles.

Thursday 11th June
Fresh gales and fair weather. Wind SE and SSE.

Birds and rock-weed showed that we were not far from land; but I expected such signs must be here, as there are many islands between the east part of Timor and New Guinea. I however hoped to fall in with Timor every hour, for I had great apprehensions that some of my people could not hold out. An extreme weakness, swelled legs, hollow and ghastly countenances, great propensity to sleep, with an apparent debility of understanding, seemed to me melancholy presages of their approaching dissolution. The surgeon and Lebogue, in particular were most miserable objects. I occasionally gave them a few teaspoonfuls of wine, out of the little I had saved for this dreadful stage, which no doubt greatly helped to support them.

For my own part, a great share of spirits, with the hopes of being able to accomplish the voyage, seemed to be my principal support; but the boatswain very innocently told me that he really thought I looked worse than anyone in the boat. The simplicity with which he uttered such an opinion diverted me, and I had good humour enough to return him a better compliment.

Every one received his 25th of a pound of bread, and quarter of a pint of water, at evening, morning, and noon, and an extra allowance of water was given to those who desired it.

At noon I observed in latitude 9° 41´ S; course S 77° W; distance 109 miles; longitude made 13° 49´ W. I had little doubt of having now passed the meridian of the eastern part of Timor, which is laid down in 128° E. This diffused universal joy and satisfaction.

Friday 12th June
Fresh breezes and fine weather, but very hazy. Wind from E to SE.

All the afternoon we had several gannets and many other birds about us, that indicated we were near land, and at sunset we kept a very anxious look-out. In the evening we caught a booby, which I reserved for our dinner the next day.

At three in the morning, with an excess of joy, we discovered Timor bearing from WSW to WNW, and I hauled on a wind to the NNE till daylight, when the land bore from SW by S about 2 leagues to NE by N 7 leagues.

It is not possible for me to describe the pleasure which the blessing of the sight of land diffused among us. It appeared scarce credible that in an open boat, and so poorly provided, we should have been able to reach the coast of Timor in 41 days after leaving Tofoa, having in that time run, by our log, a distance of 3,618 miles, and that, notwithstanding our extreme distress, no one should have perished in the voyage.

I have already mentioned, that I knew not where the Dutch settlement was situated; but I had a faint idea that it was at the SW part of the island. I therefore, after daylight, bore away along shore to the SSW, and the more readily as the wind would not suffer us to go towards the NE without great loss of time.

The day gave us a most agreeable prospect of the land, which was interspersed with woods and lawns; the interior part mountainous, but the shore low. Towards noon the coast became higher, with some remarkable headlands. We were greatly delighted with the general look of the country, which exhibited many cultivated spots and beautiful situations; but we could only see a few small huts, whence I concluded no European resided in this part of the island. Much sea ran on the shore, so that landing with a boat was impracticable. At noon I was abreast of a very high headland; the extremes of the land bore S W 1/2 W, and NNE 1/2 E; our distance off shore being three miles; latitude, by observation, 9° 59′ S; and my longitude, by dead reckoning, from the north part of New Holland, 15° 6′ W.

With the usual allowance of bread and water for dinner, I divided the bird we had caught the night before, and to the surgeon and Lebogue I gave a little wine.

Saturday 13th June

Fresh gales at E, and ESE, with very hazy weather.

During the afternoon, we continued our course along a low woody shore, with innumerable palm-trees, called the Fan Palm from the leaf spreading like a fan; but we had now lost all signs of cultivation, and the country had not so fine an appearance as it had to the eastward. This, however, was only a small tract, for by sunset it improved again, and I saw several great smokes where the inhabitants were clearing and cultivating their grounds. We had now ran 25 miles to the WSW since noon, and were W five miles from a low point, which in the afternoon I imagined had been the southernmost land, and here the coast formed a deep bend, with low land in the bight that appeared like islands. The west shore was high; but from this part of the coast to the high cape which we were abreast of yesterday noon, the shore is low, and I believe shoal. I particularly remark this situation, because here the very high ridge of mountains, that run from the east end of the island, terminate, and the appearance of the country suddenly changes for the worse, as if it was not the same island in any respect.

That we might not run past any settlement in the night, I determined to preserve my station till the morning, and therefore hove to under a close-reefed fore-sail, with which the boat lay very quiet. We were here in shoal water; our distance from the shore being half a league, the westernmost land in sight bearing WSW 1/2 W. Served bread and water for supper, and the boat lying too very well, all but the officer of the watch endeavoured to get a little sleep.

At two in the morning, we wore, and stood in shore till daylight, when I found we had drifted, during the night, about 3 leagues to the WSW, the southernmost land in sight bearing W. On examining the coast, and not seeing any sign of a settlement, we bore away to the westward, having a strong gale, against a weather current, which occasioned much sea. The shore was high and covered with wood, but we did not run far before low land again formed the coast, the points of which opening at west, I once more fancied we were on the south part of the island; but at 10 o'clock we found the coast again inclining towards the south, part of it bearing WSW 1/2 W. At the same time high land appeared from SW to SW by W 1/2 W; but the weather was so hazy, that it was doubtful whether the two lands were separated, the opening only extending one point of the compass. I, for this reason, stood towards the outer land, and found it to be the island Roti.

I returned to the shore I had left, and in a sandy bay I brought to a grapnel, that I might more conveniently calculate my situation. In this place we saw several smokes, where the natives were clearing their grounds. During the little time we remained here, the master and carpenter very much importuned me to let them go in search of supplies; to which, at length, I assented; but, finding no one willing to be of their party, they did not choose to quit the boat. I stopped here no longer than for the purpose just mentioned, and we continued steering along shore. We had a view of a beautiful-looking country, as if formed by art into lawns and parks. The coast is low, and covered with woods, in which are innumerable fan palm-trees, that look like coconut walks. The interior part is high land, but very different from the more eastern parts of the island, where it is exceedingly mountainous, and to appearance the soil better.

At noon, the island Roti bore SW by W 7 leagues. I had no observation for the latitude, but, by account, we were in 10° 12′ S; our course since yesterday noon being S 77 W, 54 miles. The usual allowance of bread and water was served for breakfast and dinner, and to the surgeon and Lebogue, I gave a little wine.

Sunday 14th June

A strong gale at ESE, with hazy weather, all the afternoon; after which the wind became moderate.

At 2 o'clock this afternoon, having run through a very dangerous breaking sea, the cause of which I attributed to a strong tide setting to windward, and shoal water, we discovered a spacious bay or sound, with a fair entrance about two or three miles wide. I now conceived hopes that our voyage was nearly at an end, as no place could appear more eligible for shipping, or more likely to be chosen for an European settlement: I therefore came to a grapnel near the east side of the entrance, in a small sandy bay, where we saw a hut, a dog, and some cattle; and I immediately sent the boatswain and gunner away to the hut, to discover the inhabitants.

The SW point of the entrance bore W 1/2 S three miles; the SE point S by W three quarters of a mile; and the island Roti from S by W 1/4 W to SW 1/4 W, about 5 leagues.

While we lay here I found the ebb came from the northward, and before our departure the falling of the tide discovered to us a reef of rocks, about two cables length from the shore; the whole being covered at high-water, renders it dangerous. On the opposite shore also appeared very high breakers; but there is nevertheless plenty of room, and certainly a safe channel for a first-rate man of war.

The bay or sound within, seemed to be of a considerable extent; the northern part, which I had now in view, being about 5 leagues distant. Here the land made in moderate risings joined by lower grounds. But the island Roti, which lies to the southward, is the best mark to know this place.

I had just time to make these remarks, when I saw the boatswain and gunner returning with some of the natives. I therefore no longer doubted of our success, and that our most sanguine expectations would be fully gratified. They brought five Indians, and informed me that they had found two families, where the women treated them with European politeness. From these people I learned, that the governor resided at a place called Coupang, which was some distance to the NE. I made signs for one of them to go in the boat, and show me Coupang, intimating that I would pay him for his trouble; the man readily complied, and came into the boat.

These people were of a dark tawny colour, and had long black hair; they chewed a great deal of beetle, and wore a square piece of cloth round their hips, in the folds of which was stuck a large knife. They had a handkerchief wrapped round their heads, and at their shoulders hung another tied by the four corners, which served as a bag for their beetle equipage.

They brought us a few pieces of dried turtle, and some ears of Indian corn. This last was most welcome to us; for the turtle was so hard, that it could not be eaten without being first soaked in hot water. Had I staid they would have brought us something more; but, as the pilot was willing, I was determined to push on. It was about half an hour past four when we sailed.

By direction of the pilot we kept close to the east shore under all our sail; but as night came on, the wind died away, and we were obliged to try at the oars, which I was surprised to see we could use with some effect. However, at 10 o'clock, as I found we got but little ahead, I came to a grapnel, and for the first time I issued double allowance of bread and a little wine to each person.

At 1 o'clock in the morning, after the most happy and sweet sleep that ever men had, we weighed, and continued to keep the east shore on board, in very smooth water; when at last I found we were again open to the sea, the whole of the land to the westward, that we had passed, being an island, which the pilot called Pulo Samow. The northern entrance of this channel is about a mile and a half or two miles wide, and I had no ground at ten fathoms.

Hearing the report of two cannon that were fired gave new life to everyone; and soon after we discovered two square-rigged vessels and a cutter at anchor to the eastward. I endeavoured to work to windward, but we were obliged to take to our oars again, having lost ground on each tack. We kept close to the shore, and continued rowing till 4 o'clock, when I brought to a grapnel, and gave another allowance of bread and wine to all hands. As soon as we had rested a little, we weighed again, and rowed till near daylight, when I came to a grapnel, off a small fort and town, which the pilot told me was Coupang.

Among the things which the boatswain had thrown into the boat before we left the ship was a bundle of signal flags that had been made for the boats to show the depth of water in sounding; with these I had, in the course of the passage, made a small jack, which I now hoisted in the main shrouds, as a signal of distress; for I did not choose to land without leave.

Soon after daybreak a soldier hailed me to land, which I instantly did, among a crowd of Indians, and was agreeably surprised to meet with an English sailor, who belonged to one of the vessels in the road. His captain, he told me, was the second person in the town; I therefore desired to be conducted to him, as I was informed the governor was ill, and could not then be spoken with.

Captain Spikerman received me with great humanity. I informed him of our miserable situation; and requested that care might be taken of those who were with me, without delay. On which he gave directions for their immediate reception at his own house, and went himself to the governor, to know at what time I could be permitted to see him; which was fixed to be at 11 o'clock.

I now desired everyone to come on shore, which was as much as some of them could do, being scarce able to walk: they, however, got at last to the house, and found tea with bread and butter provided for their breakfast.

The abilities of a painter, perhaps, could never have been displayed to more advantage than in the delineation of the two groups of figures, which at this time presented themselves. An indifferent spectator would have been at a loss which most to admire; the eyes of famine sparkling at immediate relief, or the horror of their preservers at the sight of so many spectres, whose ghastly countenances, if the cause had been unknown, would rather have excited terror than pity. Our bodies were nothing but skin and bones, our limbs were full of sores, and we were clothed in rags; in this condition, with the tears of joy and gratitude flowing down our cheeks, the people of Timor beheld us with a mixture of horror, surprise, and pity.

The governor, Mr William Adrian Van Este, notwithstanding his extreme ill-health, became so anxious about us, that I saw him before the appointed time. He received me with great affection, and gave me the fullest proofs that he was possessed of every feeling of a humane and good man. Sorry as he was, he said, that such a calamity could ever have happened to us, yet he considered it as the greatest blessing of his life that we had fallen under his protection; and, though his infirmity was so great that he could not do the office of a friend himself, he would give such orders as I might be certain would procure me every supply I wanted. In the meantime a house was hired for me, and, till matters could be properly regulated, victuals for everyone were ordered to be dressed at his own house. With respect to my people, he said I might have room for them either at the hospital or on board of Captain Spikerman's ship, which lay in the road; and he expressed much uneasiness that Coupang could not afford them better accommodations, the house assigned to me being the only one uninhabited, and the situation of the few families such that they could not accommodate anyone. After this conversation an elegant repast was set before me, more according to the custom of the country than with design to alleviate my hunger: so that in this instance he happily blended, with common politeness, the greatest favour I could receive.

On returning to my people, I found every kind relief had been given to them. The surgeon had dressed their sores, and the cleaning of their persons had not been less attended to, besides several friendly gifts of apparel.

I now desired to be shewn to the house that was intended for me, and I found it ready, with servants to attend, and a particular one which the governor had directed to be always about my person. The house consisted of a hall, with a room at each end, and a loft overhead; and was surrounded by a piazza, with an outer apartment in one corner, and a communication from the back part of the house to the street. I therefore determined, instead of separating from my people, to lodge them all with me; and I divided the house as follows: one room I took to myself, the other I allotted to the master, surgeon, Mr Nelson, and the gunner; the loft to the other officers; and the outer apartment to the men. The hall was common to the officers, and the men had the back piazza. Of this I informed the governor, and he sent down chairs, tables and benches, with bedding and other necessaries for the use of everyone.

The governor, when I took my leave, had desired me to acquaint him with everything of which I stood in need; but I was now informed it was only at particular times that he had a few moments of ease, or could attend to anything; being in a dying state, with an incurable disease. On this account, whatever business I had to transact would be with Mr Timotheus Wanjon, the second of this place, and the governor's son-in-law; who now also was contributing everything in his power to make our situation comfortable. I had been, therefore, misinformed by the seaman, who told me that Captain Spikerman was the next person to the governor.

At noon a very handsome dinner was brought to the house, which was sufficient to make persons more accustomed to plenty eat too much. Cautions, therefore, might be supposed to have had little effect; but I believe few people in such a situation would have observed more moderation. My greatest apprehension was, that they would eat too much fruit.

Having seen everyone enjoy this meal of plenty, I dined with Mr Wanjon; but I found no extraordinary inclination to eat or drink. Rest and quiet, I considered, as more necessary to my doing well, and therefore retired to my room, which I found furnished with every convenience. But, instead of rest, my mind was disposed to reflect on our late sufferings, and on the failure of the expedition; but, above all, on the thanks due to Almighty God, who had given us power to support and bear such heavy calamities, and had enabled me at last to be the means of saving eighteen lives.

In times of difficulty there will generally arise circumstances that bear more particularly hard on a commander. In our late situation, it was not the least of my distresses, to be constantly assailed with the melancholy demands of my people for an increase of allowance, which it grieved me to refuse.

The necessity of observing the most rigid economy in the distribution of our provisions was so evident that I resisted their solicitations, and never deviated from the agreement we made at setting out. The consequence of this care was that at our arrival we had still remaining sufficient for eleven days, at our scanty allowance: and if we had been so unfortunate as to have missed the Dutch settlement at Timor, we could have proceeded to Java, where I was certain every supply we wanted could be procured.

Another disagreeable circumstance, to which my situation exposed me, was the caprice of ignorant people. Had I been incapable of acting, they would have carried the boat on shore as soon as we made the island of Timor, without considering that landing among the natives, at a distance from the European settlement, might have been as dangerous as among any other Indians.

The quantity of provisions with which we left the ship was not more than we should have consumed in five days, had there been no necessity for husbanding our stock. The mutineers must naturally have concluded that we could have no other place of refuge than the Friendly Islands; for it was not likely they should imagine that, so poorly equipped as we were in every respect, there could have been a possibility of our attempting to return homewards: much less will they suspect that the account of their villainy has already reached their native country.

When I reflect how providentially our lives were saved at Tofoa by the Indians delaying their attack, and that, with scarce anything to support life, we crossed a sea of more than 1,200 leagues, without shelter from the inclemency of the weather;

when I reflect that in an open boat, with so much stormy weather, we escaped foundering, that not any of us were taken off by disease, that we had the great good fortune to pass the unfriendly natives of other countries without accident, and at last happily to meet with the most friendly and best of people to relieve our distresses; I say, when I reflect on all these wonderful escapes, the remembrance of such great mercies enables me to bear, with resignation and chearfulness, the failure of an expedition, the success of which I had so much at heart, and which was frustrated at a time when I was congratulating myself on the fairest prospect of being able to complete it in a manner that would fully have answered the intention of His Majesty, and the honourable promoters of so benevolent a plan.

With respect to the preservation of our health, during a course of 16 days of heavy and almost continual rain, I would recommend to every one in a similar situation the method we practised, which is to dip their clothes in the salt-water, and wring them out, as often as they become filled with rain; it was the only resource we had, and I believe was of the greatest service to us, for it felt more like a change of dry clothes than could well be imagined. We had occasion to do this so often, that at length all our clothes were wrung to pieces: for, except the few days we passed on the coast of New Holland, we were continually wet either with rain or sea.

Thus, through the assistance of Divine Providence, we surmounted the difficulties and distresses of a most perilous voyage, and arrived safe in an hospitable port, where every necessary and comfort were administered to us with a most liberal hand.

1st July

As, from the great humanity and attention of the governor, and the gentlemen, at Coupang, we received every kind of assistance, we were not long without evident signs of returning health: therefore, to secure my arrival at Batavia, before the October fleet sailed for Europe, on the first of July, I purchased a small schooner; 34 feet long, for which I gave 1,000 rix-dollars, and fitted her for sea, under the name of His Majesty's Schooner *Resource*.

20th July

On the 20th of July, I had the misfortune to lose Mr David Nelson: he died of an inflammatory fever. The loss of this honest man I very much lamented: he had accomplished, with great care and diligence, the object for which he was sent, and was always ready to forward every plan I proposed, for the good of the service we were on. He was equally useful in our voyage hither, in the course of which he gave me great satisfaction, by the patience and fortitude with which he conducted himself.

21st July

This day I was employed attending the funeral of Mr Nelson. The corpse was carried by twelve soldiers dressed in black, preceded by the minister; next followed myself and second governor; then ten gentlemen of the town and the officers of the ships in the harbour; and after them my own officers and people.

After reading our burial-service, the body was interred behind the chapel, in the burying-ground appropriated to the Europeans of the town. I was sorry I could get no tombstone to place over his remains.

This was the second voyage Mr Nelson had undertaken to the South Seas, having been sent out by Sir Joseph Banks; to collect plants, seeds, etc in Captain Cook's last voyage. And now, after surmounting so many difficulties, and in the midst of thankfulness for his deliverance, he was called upon to pay the debt of nature, at a time least expected.

20th August

After taking an affectionate leave of the hospitable and friendly inhabitants, I embarked, and we sailed from Coupang, exchanging salutes with the fort and shipping as we ran out of the harbour.

I left the governor, Mr Van Este, at the point of death. To this gentleman our most grateful thanks are due, for the humane and friendly treatment that we have received from him. His ill state of health only prevented him from showing us more particular marks of attention. Unhappily, it is to his memory only that I now pay this tribute. It was a fortunate circumstance for us, that Mr Wanjon, the next in place to the governor, was equally humane and ready to relieve us. His attention was unremitting, and, when there was a doubt about supplying me with money, on government account, to enable me to purchase a vessel, he cheerfully took it upon himself; without which, it was evident, I should have been too late at Batavia to have sailed for Europe with the October fleet. I can only return such services by ever retaining a grateful remembrance of them.

Mr Max, the town surgeon, likewise behaved to us with the most disinterested humanity: he attended everyone with the utmost care; for which I could not prevail on him to receive any payment, or to render me any account, or other answer, than that it was his duty.

Coupang is situated in 10° 12´ S latitude, and 124° 41´ E longitude.

29th August

On the 29th of August I passed by the west end of the Island Flores, through a dangerous strait full of islands and rocks; and, having got into the latitude of 8° S, I steered to the west, passing the islands Sumbawa, Lombock, and Bali, towards Java, which I saw on the 6th of September. I continued my course to the west, through the Straits of Madura.

September 1789

On the 10th of September I anchored off Passourwang, in latitude 7° 36´ S, and 1° 44´ W of Cape Sandana, the NE end or Java.

On the 11th I sailed, and on the 13th arrived at Sourabya, latitude 7° 11´ S, 1° 52´ west.

On the 17th of September, sailed from Sourabya, and the same day anchored at Crissey, for about two hours, and from thence I proceeded to Samarang. Latitude of Crissey 7° 9´ S, 1° 55´ west.

On the 22nd of September, anchored at Samarang; latitude 6° 54´ S; 4° 7´ W. And on the 26th I sailed for Batavia, where I arrived on the 1st of October. Latitude 6° 10´ S; 8° 12´ W from the east end of Java.

On the day after my arrival, having gone through some fatigue in adjusting matters to get my people out of the schooner, as she lay in the river, and in an unhealthy situation, I was seized with a violent fever.

October 1789

On the 7th I was carried into the country, to the physician-general's house, where, the governor-general informed me, I should be accommodated with every attendance and convenience; and to this only can I attribute my recovery. It was, however, necessary for me to quit Batavia without delay; and the governor, on that account, gave me leave, with two others, to go in a packet that was to sail before the fleet; and assured me, that those who remained should be sent after me by the fleet, which was to sail before the end of the month: that if I remained, which would be highly hazardous, he could not send us all in one ship. My sailing, therefore, was eligible, even if it had not been necessary for my health; and for that reason I embarked in the Vlydt packet, which sailed on the 16th of October.

December 1789

On the 16th of December I arrived at the Cape of Good Hope where I first observed that my usual health was returning; but for a long time I continued very weak and infirm.

I received the greatest attention and politeness from the governor-general, and all the residents on the coast of Java; and particular marks of friendship and regard from the governor, M. Van de Graaf, at the Cape of Good Hope.

On the 2nd of January, 1790, we sailed for Europe, and on the 14th of March, I was landed at Portsmouth by an Isle of Wight boat.

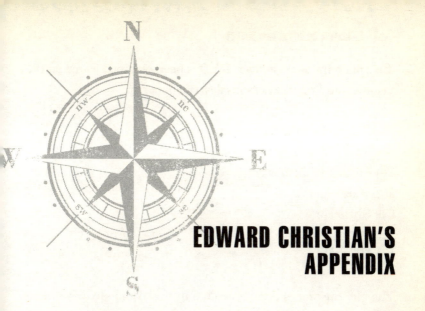

EDWARD CHRISTIAN'S
APPENDIX

To Stephen Barney Esquire, Portsmouth

Gray's-Inn Square, May 15th, 1794.

Sir,

I assure you I regard the publication of your minutes of the court-martial as a very great favour done to myself, and I am the more sensible of the obligation from being convinced that they were not originally taken with an intent to publish. But they appear to be so full and satisfactory; that, from your further kindness in permitting the extraordinary information which I have collected to be annexed as an Appendix, the public, I trust, will at length be possessed of a complete knowledge of the real causes and circumstances of that most melancholy event, the mutiny on board the *Bounty*. It is unnecessary for me to add, that I alone am responsible for the authenticity, or rather accuracy, of the information contained in the Appendix, as far at least as it has been obtained by me, in the manner and from the persons described therein.

I have the honour to be,
Sir,
Your most obedient,
and obliged servant,
Ed. Christian

THE APPENDIX

The circumstances communicated in this Appendix have been collected by a person nearly related to Christian: and it is far from his intention or wish to insinuate a vindication of the crime which has been committed. Justice, as well as policy, requires that mutiny, from whatever causes produced, or with whatever circumstances accompanied, should be punished with inexorable rigour. The publication of the trial, and of these extraordinary facts, it is presumed, will in no degree impede the pursuit of justice, yet it will administer some consolation to the broken hearts, which this melancholy transaction has occasioned. And whilst the innocent families and relations of twenty-one unhappy men are deeply interested in reducing to its just measure the infamy which this dreadful act has brought upon them; every friend to truth and strict justice must feel his attention awakened to the true causes and circumstances, which have hitherto been concealed or misrepresented, of one of the most remarkable events in the annals of the navy. It is the aim of the writer of this Appendix to state facts as they are, and to refrain, as far as possible, from invective and reproach.

It will naturally be asked from whom, and how have these facts been collected? And why have they been so long suppressed? It may be answered, that the writer of this Appendix, with the other relations of the mutineers, entertained no distrust of the narratives published to the world, or the accounts which they received in private; and as they came from those whose sufferings had unquestionably been extreme, and preservation almost miraculous; and thus carrying with them the stamp of even greater authenticity than the solemn declarations of a death-bed, they precluded all suspicion and enquiries among those who were most concerned in the horrid representation. Their lips were closed, they mourned in silence, and shuddering at the most distant allusion to this melancholy subject, they were of all persons the least likely to discover the real truth of the transaction.

All the circumstances stated here could not be produced at the trial, as the Court confined the witnesses, as much as possible, to the question, 'Who were actually engaged in the mutiny?' for that being a crime which will admit of no legal justification, the relation or previous circumstances could not be material or legal evidence, yet what passed at the time of the mutiny was so immediately connected with what had happened previously in the ship, that in the testimony of most of the witnesses there will be found an allusion to, or confirmation of, what is here advanced.

Some time after the trial of the mutineers, the writer of this Appendix received such information as surprised him greatly, and in consequence of which, he resolved to make every possible enquiry into this unhappy affair. The following circumstances have been collected from many interviews and conversations, in the presence and hearing of several respectable gentlemen, with

Mr Fryer,[1] master of the *Bounty*; Mr Hayward,[2] midshipman; Mr Peckover,[3] gunner; Mr Purcell,[4] carpenter; John Smith,[5] cook; Lawrence Lebogue,[6] sail maker; all these returned in the boat with Captain Bligh: and with Joseph Coleman,[7] armourer; Thomas McIntosh,[8] carpenter's mate; Michael Byrne,[9] seaman; these are three of the four, who were tried and honourably acquitted, even with Captain Bligh's testimony in their favour; and with Mr Haywood, midshipman, who has received His Majesty's pardon; and William Musprat, discharged by the opinion of the judges in his favour; upon a point of evidence: the writer of this has received letters also upon the subject from James Morrison, the boatswain's mate; who was pardoned. Mr Haywood is now serving again as midshipman, under Lord Howe, in the *Queen Charlotte*, and is much respected by all who know him, and Morrison and Musprat are also employed again in the king's service; yet the writer of this Appendix thinks it necessary to assure the reader that no material fact here stated stands in need of their testimony or confirmation. The gentlemen who were present at different conversations with the persons just mentioned, are; John Farhill, Esq. No 38, Mortimer Street; Samuel Romilly, Esq. Lincoln's Inn; Mr Gilpin, No 432, Strand;

---

1 Now of the *Inconstant* man of war.
2 Now Lieutenant in the *Diomede*, East Indies.
3 Lives at No. 13, Gun Alley, Wapping.
4 Now of the *Dromedary*, West Indies.
5 In London, but residence unknown.
6 In Greenwich Hospital.
7 In ditto.
8 In the merchants' service, his mother keeps a public house at North Shields.
9 In Greenwich Hospital.

the Rev Dr Fisher, Canon of Windsor; the Rev Mr Cookson, Canon of Windsor; Captain Wordsworth, of the Abergavenny East Indiaman; Rev Mr Antrobus, Chaplain to the Bishop of London; John France, Esq. Temple; James Losh, Esq. Temple; Rev Dr Frewen, Colchester; and John Atkinson, Esq. Somerset Herald. Each of these gentlemen has heard the declarations of one at the least of the persons before mentioned; some have had an interview with five or six of them at different times, together with the writer of this Appendix, who is confident that everyone of these gentlemen will bear testimony that what he has heard is not here exaggerated or misrepresented. There is no contradiction or variance whatever, in the account given by the gentlemen and people of the *Bounty*, though they could not upon every occasion be all present together, and therefore cannot all relate exactly the same circumstances.

They declare that Captain Bligh used to call his officers 'scoundrels, damned rascals, hounds, hell-hounds, beasts, and infamous wretches'; that he frequently threatened them, that when the ship arrived at Endeavor Straits, 'he would kill one half of the people, make the officers jump overboard, and would make them eat grass like cows'; and that Christian, and Stewart, another midshipman, were as much afraid of Endeavour Straits, as any child is of a rod.

Captain Bligh was accustomed to abuse Christian much more frequently and roughly than the rest of the officers, or as one of the persons expressed it, 'whatever fault was found, Mr Christian was sure to bear the brunt of the Captain's anger.' In speaking to him in this violent manner, Captain Bligh frequently 'shook his fist in Christian's face.' But the immediate cause of the melancholy event is attributed to what happened on the 26th and 27th of April; the mutiny broke out on the morning of the 28th of April 1789. The *Bounty* had stopped at Annamooko, one of the Friendly Islands; on the 26th Christian was sent upon a watering party, with express orders from the Captain, by no means to fire upon the natives; upon their return, the Captain was informed that the natives had stolen the cooper's adze; at this Captain Bligh was in a great rage, and abused Christian much; saying to him, 'Goddamn your blood, why did not you fire, you an officer!'

At this island the Captain and ship's company had bought quantities of coconuts, at the rate of 20 for a nail; the Captain's heap lay upon deck, and on the morning of the 27th, Captain Bligh fancied that the number was diminished, but the master, Mr Fryer, told him he supposed they were pressed closer from being run over by the men in the night. The Captain then ordered the officer of the morning watch, Mr Christian, to be called; when he came, the Captain accosted him thus, 'Damn your blood, you have stolen my coconuts'; Christian answered, 'I was dry, I thought it of no consequence, I took one only, and I am sure no one touched another.' Captain Bligh then replied, 'You lie, you scoundrel, you have stolen one half.' Christian appeared much hurt and agitated, and said, 'Why do you treat me thus, Captain Bligh?' Captain Bligh then shook his hand in his face and said, 'No reply'; and called him 'a thief', and other abusive names. He then ordered the quarter-masters to go down and bring all the coconuts both from man and officer, and put them upon the quarter deck. They were brought. The Captain then called all hands upon deck, and desired 'the people to look after the officers, and the officers to look after the people, for there never were such a set of damned thieving rascals under any man's command in the world before.' And he told the men, 'You are allowed a pound and a half of yams today, but tomorrow I shall reduce you to three quarters of a pound.' All declare that the ship's company were before greatly discontented at their short allowance of provisions, and their discontent was increased from the consideration that they had plenty of provisions on board, and that the Captain was his own purser[1].

About 4 o'clock on the same day, Captain Bligh abused Christian again. Christian came forward from Captain Bligh, crying, 'tears were running fast from his eyes in big drops.' Purcell, the Carpenter, said to him, 'What is the matter Mr Christian?' He said, 'Can you ask me, and hear the treatment I receive?' Purcell replied, 'Do not I receive as bad as you do?' Christian said, 'You have something[2] to protect you, and can speak again; but if I should speak to him as you do, he would probably break me, turn me before the mast, and perhaps flog me; and if he did, it would be the death of us both, for I am sure I should take him in my arms, and jump overboard with him.' Purcell said, 'Never mind it, it is but for a short time longer.' Christian said, 'In going through Endeavour Straits, I am sure the ship will be a hell.' He was heard by another person to say, when he was crying, 'I would rather die ten thousand deaths, than bear this treatment; I always do my duty as an officer and as a man ought to do, yet I receive this scandalous usage.' Another person

1 During the mutiny, Captain Bligh said to Mr Young, 'This is a serious affair, Mr Young.' Mr Young replied, 'Yes, it is a serious affair to be starved, I hope this day to get a belly full.'

2 By this he meant his warrant; the warrant-officers can only be punished by suspension and confinement, they cannot be broke and flogged like midshipmen.

heard him say, 'That flesh and blood cannot bear this treatment.' This was the only time he ever was seen in tears on board the ship; and one of the seamen being asked, if he had ever observed Christian in tears before, answered, 'No, he was no milksop.'

It is now certainly known, that Christian after this had prepared to leave the ship that night upon a raft; those who came with Captain Bligh can only know it by circumstances, which they afterwards recollected, and which were the subject of conversation in the boat. He gave away that afternoon all his Otaheite curiosities; he was seen tearing his letters and papers, and throwing them overboard; he applied to the carpenter for nails, who told him to take as many as he pleased out of the locker; and the ship intending to stop at no other island, these could have been of no use to him, but in case of his escape to land. Mr Tinkler, a young boy, one of Christian's messmates, was hungry in the evening, and went below to get some pig which was left at dinner; this he missed, and after some search, found it packed up with a breadfruit, in a dirty clothes bag in Christian's cot; when the launch was hoisted out, the two masts were lashed to a plank, which they were obliged to untie. This was the raft or stage upon which he intended to leave the ship.

These circumstances are remembered by those who came in the boat, but his design of going off upon the raft was frequently the subject of conversation afterwards in the ship. Norman, one of the four who were honourably acquitted, said to him after the mutiny, 'this is a hard case upon me, Mr Christian, who have a wife and family in England.'[3] Christian replied, 'It is a hard case, Norman, but it never would have happened, if

---

3 Norman's family live at Portsmouth.

I could have left the ship alone.' Christian told them afterwards on the ship, 'that he did not expect to reach the shore upon the raft, but he was in hopes of being seen and taken up by some of the natives in their canoes.' The reason of his disappointment is said to have been owing to the people being upon deck in greater numbers than usual, looking at a volcano in the island of Tofoa.

All agree that there was no plot or intention to mutiny before Christian went upon his watch, at four in the morning. The mutiny broke out at 5 o'clock, and all the mutineers were in bed when it began, except those who were in Christian's watch; how soon after 4 o'clock the conspiracy was entered into, before it was put in execution, does not appear. That there had been some agreement previous to the breaking out of the mutiny is manifest from the evidence of Mr Fryer, who was told by two of them, 'Sir, there is no one means to hurt you; no, that was our agreement, not to commit murder.' This statement cannot be reconciled with the testimony of Mr Hayward and Mr Hallet, who were both in Christian's watch; if the reader were not apprised of a circumstance which was not mentioned before the court-martial; viz that these gentlemen who were very young at that time, viz about fifteen, had both fallen asleep. The circumstance of the rest of the mutineers being in bed when the mutiny began, proves that it had not been preconcerted with them; and it is remarkable that Mr Young was the only person among Christian's messmates who was concerned in it, and he was in bed when it broke out. On the 26th, before the ship left Annamooko, Christian and some other officers threw away their beads and trifles among the natives, as articles for which they would have no further occasion.

It appears from the testimony of every witness, that the original intent was to put the Captain on shore, with three other persons only, and if the smallest boat, which was hoisted out for that purpose, had not been leakey, it is probable that this design would have been carried into execution; but by the time that the second cutter or boat was got into the water, a great number desired to leave the ship, and requested the launch. It is agreed by all that every person who went into the launch went voluntarily, or might have continued on board if he had wished to stay, except the four who were first ordered into the small boat; and afterwards Mr Fryer, who was commanded to go in consequence of his design to retake the ship being overheard. It is indeed expressly proved by Mr Hallet, that 'the boatswain and carpenters told Christian, they would prefer going in the boat, to staying in the ship; and he said he did not wish them, or any other, to stay against their inclination, or to go; and that the most part went voluntarily.' And Mr Hayward in his evidence has also deposed, 'I heard no one ordered to go into the boat, but Mr Hallet, Mr Samuel, and myself.' Although Mr Fryer himself wished to stay, from a very laudable motive, viz that of retaking the ship; yet being obliged to go, he earnestly requested that his brother-in-law, Tinkler, then a young boy, might be permitted to follow him.[1] In such a dilemma, the alternative was dreadful, yet those who went voluntarily into the launch were sure of getting to shore, where they expected to live, until a European ship

---

1 It is worthy of notice that Lambe the butcher was a mutineer; but when he saw such a number going off in the launch, he actually laid down his arms and joined them; he afterwards died at Batavia.

Martin, another mutineer, attempted to get into the launch, but was opposed by the carpenter, who said he would get him hanged when they got to England; and he was then ordered back by the people in the ship.

arrived, or until they could raise their boat or build a greater, as one of the mutineers said of the carpenter, 'you might as well give him the ship as his tool chest.' It is proved by Mr Hallet, that they were veered astern, in order to be towed towards the land, which was so near, that it is said they might see them reach the shore from the mast-head of the ship.

After the mutiny commenced it was between three and four hours before the launch left the ship, and one reason, besides the number of persons, why she was so deeply laden, was, that almost all Captain Bligh's property in boxes and trunks was put on board. A short time after it had quitted the ship, Christian declared, that 'he would readily sacrifice his own life, if the persons in the launch were all safe in the ship again.'

At Annamooko, besides the cooper's adze being stolen, the natives, by diving, had cut and carried off a grapnel by which a boat was fastened. Captain Bligh, in order to compel the natives to restore it, had made them believe he would sail away with their chiefs whom he had on board; this was unattended with success, as they assured him the grapnel had been carried away in a canoe belonging to another island; but the people of the island, who crowded round the ship to entreat the deliverance of their chiefs, and the chiefs themselves, were greatly frightened and distressed, before they were set at liberty. For Captain Bligh carried them out some distance to sea, and they were followed and taken back in canoes.[1] This unfortunate circumstance is

---

1 When Mr Nelson told Mr Peckover that the ship is taken from us, Mr Peckover in evidence says, he answered, 'We were a long way from land when I came off deck' (thinking, as he declares, that the people in the canoes had followed and taken the ship); and so it was understood by Mr Nelson, who replies, 'It is by our own people.'

supposed to have been the cause of the rough reception which the people in the launch met with at Tofoa. For Nageete, one of the chiefs, who had been thus frightened, had come upon a visit from Annamooko, though 10 leagues distant, and was one of the first persons they saw at Tofoa. He appeared at the first friendly, yet it is thought that he was glad of having this opportunity of resenting the treatment he had received in the ship at Annamooko.

Those who came in the boat, though they gave vent to no open complaints, yet sometimes made allusions in the hearing of the Captain, to what had passed previous to the mutiny. Captain Bligh was one day observing that it was surprising that this should have happened after he had been so kind to the people by making them fine messes of wheat; upon which Mr Hallet replied, 'If it had not been for your fine messes, and fine doings, we should have had the ship for our resource[1] instead of the boat.'

In a misunderstanding about some oysters, between the Captain and the carpenter, Captain Bligh told him, 'If I had not taken so much pains with you, you would never have been here'; the carpenter replied, 'Yes, if you had not taken so much pains with us, we should never have been here.'

In the evidence of Mr Peckover and Mr Fryer, it is proved that Mr Nelson the botanist said, upon hearing the commencement of

---

1 It just be supposed that, after a distance of time, although the ideas and impressions are remembered, the exact words will be forgotten; but one person particularly recollects that Mr Hallet used the word *resource* upon this occasion, because he afterwards fancied it was thus suggested to Captain Bligh's mind, as the name which he gave to the vessel purchased at Timor.

the mutiny, 'We know whose fault this is, or who is to blame, and oh! Mr Fryer, what have we brought upon ourselves?' In addition to this, it ought to be known that Mr Nelson, in conversation afterwards with an officer at Timor, who was speaking of returning with Captain Bligh if he got another ship, observed, 'I am surprised that you should think of going a second time with one (using a term of abuse) who has been the occasion of all our losses.'

In Captain Bligh's Narrative no mention is made of the two little boats or cutters, the least boat would not hold more than six, and the larger more than nine persons. But after Captain Bligh relates that he was brought upon deck, he proceeds thus in the two next paragraphs:

'The boatswain was now ordered to hoist out the *launch*, with a threat if he did not do it instantly, to take care of himself.

'The *boat* being out, Mr Haywood and Mr Hallett, midshipmen, and Mr Samuel, were ordered into it.'

Every reader must have supposed that the boat mentioned in the latter paragraph was the same as the launch in the former, and that these four were the first of the nineteen who were ordered into it.

If the small boats had been distinctly mentioned in Captain Bligh's Narrative, it would have been manifest to all the world that the mutiny could not have been the result of a conspiracy of twenty-five of the people, to turn the other nineteen into one or both of them.

Indeed, many readers had the penetration to think that it was incredible, and almost beyond any calculation of probability, that twenty-five persons could have been seduced to have concurred in such a horrid plot, without a single one having the virtue to resist the temptation, and to disclose the design to the Captain.

In the Narrative, there is this memorable paragraph:

'Notwithstanding the roughness with which I was treated, the remembrance of past kindnesses produced some signs of remorse in Christian. When they were forcing me out of the ship, I asked him if this treatment was a proper return for the many instances he had received of my friendship? He appeared disturbed at my question, and answered with much emotion, "That, Captain Bligh, that is the thing; I am in hell – I am in hell."'

In Mr Purcell's evidence before the Court, this conversation is sworn to thus: 'Captain Bligh attempted to speak to Christian, who said, "Hold your tongue, and I'll not hurt you; it is too late to consider now, I have been in hell for weeks past with you."'

But all, who were upon deck and overheard the whole of this conversation, state it thus: 'Captain Bligh, addressing himself to Christian, said, "Consider Mr Christian, I have a wife and four children in England, and you have danced my children upon your knee." Christian replied, "You should have thought of them sooner yourself, Captain Bligh, it is too late to consider now, I have been in hell for weeks past with you."'

Christian afterwards told the people in the ship, that when Bligh spoke of his wife and children, 'my heart melted, and I would then have jumped overboard, if I could have saved you, but as it was too late to do that, I was obliged to proceed.' One person, who heard what passed immediately after Captain Bligh was brought upon deck, says, that Captain Bligh asked Christian, 'What is meaning of all this?' And Christian answered, 'Can you ask, Captain Bligh, when you know you have treated us officers, and all these poor fellows, like Turks?'

Captain Bligh in his Narrative asserts, 'When we were sent away 'Huzza for Otaheite', was frequently heard among the mutineers.' But everyone of those who came in the boat, as well as all who stayed in the ship, declare that they neither heard nor observed any huzzaing whatever in the ship.

In Captain Bligh's Narrative, there is the following paragraph:

'Had their mutiny been occasioned by any grievances, either real or imaginary, I must have discovered symptoms of their discontent, which would have put me on my guard, but the case was far otherwise. Christian in particular I was on the most friendly terms with; that very day he was engaged to have dined with me; and the preceding night he excused himself from supping with me, on pretence of being unwell; for which I felt concerned, having no suspicions of his integrity and honour.'

It is said that the Captain had his officers to dine with him in rotation, and Christian's turn might have fallen on the day of the mutiny, but in consequence of the charge of stealing the coconuts, the gentlemen (or most of them) had resolved not to dine again at the Captain's table. Mr Fryer had not dined there for a long time before. It is true that Captain Bligh had asked Christian to supper; but it now appears, he excused himself, not to meditate the destruction of his benefactor, but his own flight.

It was proved on the trial that Christian, during the mutiny, told Mr Fryer, 'You know, Mr Fryer, I have been in hell on board this ship for weeks past'; and that he said to the Captain, 'I have been in hell for weeks past with you': but what particular period Christian referred to, or when the poignancy of his distress had begun to prey upon his mind, does not appear. But instances are mentioned of Christian's being hurt by Captain Bligh's treatment, even at the Cape of Good Hope, in their outward bound voyage. Christian had the command of the tent on shore at Otaheite, where Captain sometimes entertained the Chiefs of the island, and before all the company used to abuse Christian for some pretended fault or other, and the Chiefs would afterwards take an opportunity of observing to Christian, 'Titriano, Brie worrite beha': i.e. 'Christian, Bligh is perhaps angry with you.' Christian would turn it off by saying, 'No, no.' But he afterwards complained to the officers of the Captain's cruelty in abusing him before the people of the country, observing that he would not regard it, if he would only find fault with him in private.

There is no country in the world where the notions of aristocracy and family pride are carried higher than at Otaheite; and it is a remarkable circumstance that the Chiefs are naturally distinguished by taller persons, and more open and intelligent countenances, than the people of inferior condition; hence these are the principal qualities by which the natives estimate the gentility of strangers; and Christian was so great a favourite with them that according to the words of one person, 'They adored the very ground he trod upon.' He was Tyo, or friend, to a Chief of the first rank in the island, whose name, according to the custom of the country, he took in exchange for his own; and whose property he participated. This Chief dined one day with Captain Bligh, and was told by him that 'his Tyo Christian, was only his Towtow, or servant'. The Chief upbraided Christian with this, who was much mortified at being thus degraded in the opinion of his friend, and endeavoured to recommend himself again to the Chief, by assuring him that he, Captain Bligh, and all the officers, were Towtows of the King of Bretane.

These circumstances, although comparatively trifling, are such as to be distinctly remembered, but they prove that there could be little harmony where such painful sensations were so frequently and unnecessarily excited.

A regard to truth obliges the writer of this Appendix to add that Captain Bligh has told some of Christian's relations, that after they sailed from Otaheite, Christian, when he was upon duty, had put the ship in great danger; from which Captain Bligh supposed that it had been his intention to cripple the ship, that they might be obliged to return to Otaheite to repair. But no such circumstance is remembered by any person besides the Captain.[1] Captain Bligh has also declared that the persons in the launch 'were turned out to certain destruction, because the mutineers had not the courage to embrue their hands in blood.' It has already been observed, that it is proved before the court-martial, that most of the persons went into the launch voluntarily. And it is certainly true, that, although the sufferings of the persons in the boat were distressful to the last degree, they were not the occasion of the death of Mr Nelson at Timor, or of those who died at Batavia; for all recovered from the extremity to which they had been reduced by this unhappy voyage.

It is agreed that Christian was the first to propose the mutiny, and the project of turning the Captain on shore at Tofoa, to the people in his watch, but he declared afterwards in the ship, he

---

1 They had sailed from Otaheite twenty-four days when the mutiny broke out, and as in those seas a constant trade wind blows from east to west; in order to return to Otaheite, they must have been obliged to have gone into a high southern latitude before they could have gained the advantage of the variable winds. Their return to Otaheite would probably have taken up twice or thrice twenty-four days. If the mutiny had been plotted at Otaheite, it is not probable the execution of it would have been so long delayed.

never should have thought of it, if it had not been suggested to his mind by an expression of Mr Stewart, who knowing of his intention of leaving the ship upon the raft, told him, 'when you go, Christian, we are ripe for anything.'

The mutiny is ascribed by all who remained in the ship by this unfortunate expression, which probably proceeded rather from a regard for Christian than from a mutinous disposition, for all declare that Stewart was an excellent officer, and a severe disciplinarian, severe to such a degree as to be disliked by the seamen, though much respected for his abilities. Mr Stewart was in bed when the mutiny broke out, and afterwards was neither in arms, nor active on the side of the mutineers, yet it ought not to be concealed, that during the mutiny he was dancing and clapping his hands in the Otaheite manner, and saying, 'It was the happiest day of his life.' He was drowned in the wreck of the *Pandora*. This gentleman is spoken of by all in terms of great praise and respect. He is said to have been the best practical navigator on board, even superior in that character to Captain Bligh and Christian.[1] Soon after the launch had left the ship, Christian told the people that he had no right to the command, and that he would act in any station they would assign him. But they all declared that he should be their Captain, and after some persuasion from Christian, they permitted Mr Stewart

---

1 Though all acknowledge Captain Bligh's great skill and abilities in theory, and in making observations, yet they all declare, that in the practical management of a ship he was not superior to Stewart or Christian. For the two last are thus classed and compared with the Captain. Captain Bligh was the best artist on board; Stewart the best seaman; and Christian was the best in both characters united. Stewart was several years senior to Christian, both in age and in the service.

to be the second in command, though they were desirous, from Stewart's former severity, of preferring Mr Haywood; but being told by Christian, that as the ship must be at watch and watch, he thought Mr Haywood, who was then only sixteen, too young and inexperienced for such a charge, with some reluctance they acceded to his recommendation of Mr Stewart. The other arrangements being settled, instead of insisting upon going back to Otaheite, they told Christian he might carry them wherever he thought proper. Christian advised them to go to an island called Tobooy, which was laid down in the charts by Captain Cook, though no European ship had ever landed there. This lies about seven degrees south of Otaheite, and it was chosen because it was out of the track of European ships.[1] When they arrived there, and with difficulty had made a landing, although it was full of inhabitants, they found no quadrupeds but a species of small rats, with which the island was completely overrun. They stayed there a few days, and then resolved to sail to Otaheite for a ship load of hogs, goats, dogs, cats, and fowls, to stock the island of Tobooy, which they had fixed upon for their settlement.'[2]

---

1 One of the four acquitted, said, 'Mr Christian was a fine scholar, he carried us like a shot to Tobooy, and told us within half an hour where we should make land.'

2 They prevailed upon the king to give them a bull and a cow, which were kept tied up as royal curiosities; but the voyage back to Tobooy was very tempestuous, and the bull being old could not stand upon his legs, and died in consequence of the bruises from his falls. There is a breed of English cattle, which run wild upon the mountains of Otaheite, but the natives cannot be persuaded to make use either of their flesh or milk.

When they had reached Otaheite, in order to acquire what they wanted more expeditiously, Christian told the Chiefs and people that Captain Bligh had returned to Captain Cook, who had sent Christian back to purchase for him the different articles which they wished to obtain.

This story was the more plausible, as the people of Otaheite had been told by Captain Bligh that Captain Cook was still living and that he had sent him for the breadfruit. Such is still their love and veneration for the memory of Captain Cook that the natives even contended for the honour of sending their best hogs and animals to Toote. The ship by this artifice being soon filled, they returned with some Otaheite men and women to Tobooy. It was thought that the Otaheite men would be useful in introducing them to the friendship and good offices of the natives. At Tobooy they built a fort[1], and having stayed there three months, and finding the inhabitants always inhospitable and treacherous, the people of the ship grew discontented; all hands were called up, and it being put to the vote what should be done, sixteen out of the twenty-five voted that they should go back to Otaheite. Christian, thinking that this was the general wish, said, 'Gentlemen, I will carry you, and land you wherever you please; I desire no one to stay with me, but I have one favour to request, that you will grant me the ship, tie the foresail, and give me a few gallons of water, and leave me to run

---

1 Christian having endeavoured to convince them of the necessity of building a fort for their protection, assured them that he would take his share of the labour, and calling for a pick-axe, was the first who began the operations.

before the wind, and I shall land upon the first island the ship drives to. I have done such an act that I cannot stay at Otaheite. I will never live where I may be carried home to be a disgrace to my family.'

Upon this, Mr Young, the midshipman, and seven others declared, 'We shall never leave you, Mr Christian, go where you will.' It was then agreed that the other sixteen should be landed at Otaheite, and have their share of the arms and other necessary articles; and he proposed to the rest that they should go and seek an island, not before discovered, where they were not likely to be found, and having run the ship aground, and taken out every thing of value, and scuttled and broke up the ship, they should endeavour to make a settlement. They reached Otaheite on the 27th of September 1789, and came to anchor in Matavai Bay about 11 o'clock in the forenoon, and the sixteen were disembarked with their portions of the arms and other necessaries. Christian took leave of Mr Stewart and Mr Haywood, and told them he should sail that evening; and desired them, if they ever got to England, to inform his friends and country what had been the cause of his committing so desparate an act; but to guard against any obstruction, he concealed the time of his sailing from the rest.

The natives came on board in crowds as usual, and about 12 o'clock at night he cut his cable, and sailed from the Bay. The people on board consisted of nine Englishmen, about twenty-five men, women, boys, and girls, of different ages, from Otaheite, and two men from Tobooy. It does not appear that any selection was made of the Otaheiteans, who are always eager to be carried away in an English ship. The ship was seen standing off the island the next morning, but from that day, for the nineteen months the others lived at Otaheite, they never saw nor heard anything more of Christian; and upon the arrival of Captain Edwards in the *Pandora*, they could give him no further account of the *Bounty* than what is here stated.[1]

During his short stay at Otaheite, Christian was much pressed to go on shore to visit the King, but he declined it, saying, 'How can I look him in the face, after the lie I told him when I was here last?' These circumstances concerning the *Bounty*, subsequent to the mutiny, must necessarily be collected from the seven persons who were left in the ship, and who are now, or were lately, in England. These say that Christian was always sorrowful and dejected after the mutiny; and before he left them, had become such an altered man in his looks and appearance, as to render it probable that he would not long survive this dreadful catastrophe. Indeed, it is impossible that he should have

---

1 Sixteen were left at Otaheite, one of whom, in a quarrel about their arms, was shot by another Englishman, who was put to death by the natives, as an act of justice, the other fourteen surrendered themselves to Captain Edwards, or were taken by the people of the *Pandora*; four of these were lost when the *Pandora* was shipwrecked; four have been honourably acquitted; two have received His Majesty's pardon; one has been discharged by the opinion of the judges in his favour; and the remaining three have suffered death according to the sentence of the court-martial. Millward, one of the three, was in bed when the mutiny broke out; the other two were in Christian's watch; Ellison, one of them, was a young boy at the time. When the others went down to arm themselves, he was left at the helm. He was afterwards active in the mutiny. He had got a musket in his hand, which Christian having observed, said, 'You little monkey, what business have you with that?' and ordered it to be taken from him.

appeared[1] otherwise, if he deserved the character which all unite in giving him.

In the Royal Jamaica Gazette, dated February 9, 1793, which announced the arrival of Captain Bligh in the *Providence*, the following was one of the paragraphs, and it has been copied into all the English newspapers:

'Captain Bligh could gain no intelligence of the mutineer Christian and his accomplices, who were on board the *Bounty*. When they returned to Otaheite, after executing their infernal project, the natives, suspecting some mischief from the non-appearance of the Commander and the gentlemen with him, laid a plan to seize the vessel and crew; but a *favourite female* of Christian's betrayed the design of her countrymen. He put to sea in the night, and the next morning the ship was nearly out of sight.'

It is immaterial to inquire who was the author of this paragraph, yet it cannot but be remarked that it is totally different from the account which has been given by those who stayed at Otaheite, and who can have no possible interest in

---

1 Though they say kept up good discipline in the ship, yet he was generally below, leaning his head upon his hand, and when they came down for orders, he seldom raised his head to answer more than 'Yes', or 'No'.

One of the seamen being asked if they never mutinied afterwards in the ship, and told Christian they had as good a right to the command as he had, said, 'No, no man would ever have mutinied against Mr Christian, no one ever thought of resisting his authority.'

One method, it is said, which he adopted to prevent riot and confusion in the ship, was, to draw off secretly the spirituous liquors from the casks, and he then persuaded the people they had drank them to the bottom.

concealing this circumstance, if in fact it had existed; nor can it be reconciled with probability, or the treatment and protection which the Englishmen experienced from the natives when the ship had left them.

As this paragraph contains an assertion that Christian had a *favourite female* at Otaheite, it is proper that it should be known that although Christian was upon shore, and had the command of the tent all the time that Captain Bligh was at Otaheite with the *Bounty*, yet the officers who were with Christian upon the same duty declare that he never had a female favourite at Otaheite, nor any attachment or particular connection among the women. It is true that some had what they call *their girls*, or women with whom they constantly lived all the time they were upon the island, but this was not the case with Christian.

Until this melancholy event, no young officer was ever more affectionately beloved for his amiable qualities, or more highly respected for his abilities and brave and officer-like conduct. The world has been led to suppose that the associates in his guilt were attached to him only by his seducing and diabolical villainy. But all those who came in the boat, whose sufferings and losses on his account have been so severe, not only speak of him without resentment and with forgiveness, but with a degree of rapture and enthusiasm. The following are, word for word, some of the unpremeditated expressions, used by the gentlemen and people of the *Bounty*, in speaking of this unfortunate mutineer: 'His Majesty might have his equal, but he had not a superior officer in his service.' This probably had a reference to his age, which was about twenty-three. 'He was a gentleman, and a brave man; and every officer and seaman on board the ship would have gone through fire and water to have served him.' 'He was adorned with every virtue, and beloved by all.' 'He was a gentleman every inch of him, and I would still wade up to the armpits in blood to serve him.' 'As much as I have lost and suffered by him, if he could be restored to his country, I should be the first to go without wages in search of him.' 'He was as good and as generous a man as ever lived.' 'Mr Christian was always good-natured, I never heard him say Damn you, to any man on board the ship.' 'Everybody under his command did their duty at a look from Mr Christian, and I would still go through fire and water for him.' These are respectively the expressions of nine different persons, and it is the language of one and all. Mr Hayward in his evidence, no doubt with a proper sentiment of the crime of mutiny, has used the words, 'Christian, and his gang' yet that gentleman has declared that, until the desperate act, Christian deserved the character described by the strongest of the above expressions.

Christian, having stayed at school longer than young men generally do who enter into the navy, and being allowed by all who knew him to possess extraordinary abilities, is an excellent scholar, and everyone acquainted with him from a boy, till he went on board the *Bounty*, can testify that no young man was ever more ambitious of all that is esteemed right and honourable among men, or more anxious to acquire distinction and advancement by his good conduct in his profession. He had been an acting Midshipman but a short time in the service, when Captain Courtenay, the late brave Commander of the *Boston* frigate, entrusted him with the charge of a watch in the *Eurydice* all the way home from the East Indies. This, no doubt, was extremely flattering to him, and he declared to a relation who met him at Woolwich, 'he had been extremely happy under Captain Courtenay's command'; and at the same time observed, that 'it was very easy to make one's self beloved and respected on board a ship; one had only to be always ready to obey one's superior officers, and to be kind to the common men, unless there was occasion for severity, and if you are severe when there is a just occasion, they will not like you the worse for it.'[1]

This was after the conclusion of the peace, and within a few days the ship was paid off; and being out of employ, he wished to be appointed a Mate of a West-Indiaman, a situation for which he thought himself qualified. Whilst he was in treaty with a merchant in the city to go in that capacity in his ship, Captain Taubman, a relation of Christian's, came to London from the Isle of Man, and suggested to Christian that it would be very desirable for him to serve under so experienced a navigator as Captain Bligh, who had been Sailing-Master to Captain Cook, and who was then in the merchant's service; and as Captain Taubman was acquainted with Captain Bligh, he offered to make an application to him in Christian's favour. The application was made, and Captain Bligh returned a polite answer that he was sorry he could not take Christian, having then his complement of officers. Upon this, Christian of his own accord observed that 'wages were no object, he only wished to learn his profession, and if Captain Bligh would permit him to mess with the gentlemen, he would readily enter his ship as a Foremast-man until there was a vacancy among the officers'; and at the same time added,

---

1 Christian always spoke of Captain Courtenay as an officer and a gentleman, with the greatest affection and gratitude. The gentlemen and people on board the *Eurydice*, the writer of this Appendix has been assured, declare that Christian was the last person whom they would have expected to have committed such a crime.

'we Midshipmen are gentlemen, we never pull at a rope; I should even be glad to go one voyage in that situation, for there may be occasions, when officers may be called upon to do the duties of a common man.'

To this proposal Captain Bligh had no objection, and in that character he sailed one voyage, and upon his return spoke of Captain Bligh with great respect: he said that although he had his share of labour with the common men, the Captain had been kind to him in shewing him the use of his charts and instruments; but at the same time he observed that Captain Bligh was very passionate; yet he seemed to pride himself in knowing how to humour him. In the next voyage, Captain Bligh took him out as his Second Mate, and before his return the Captain was chosen to Command the *Bounty*.[1] Christian wishing to go upon a voyage where so much service would be seen, in which he would complete his time as a Midshipman, and if it had been successful, he would, no doubt, with little difficulty upon his return have been raised to the rank of Lieutenant, was recommended to the Admiralty by Captain Bligh himself, as one of his officers; and as it was understood that great interest had been made to get Midshipmen sent out in this ship, Christian's friends thought this recommendation, as they do still, a very great obligation. Captain Bligh had no Lieutenants on board, and the ship at

---

1 Upon Christian's return from the second voyage to the West Indies with Captain Bligh, he had no opportunity of a personal interview with his friends, and he made no complaint by letter. But a person, who had sailed with Captain Bligh and Christian, both to the West Indies and the South Seas, being asked if Captain Bligh's treatment of Christian had always been the same said, 'No, it would not long have been born in the merchants service.'

the first was divided into two watches, the charge of which was entrusted to the Master and the Gunner: but after they had sailed about a month, the Captain divided the ship into three watches, and gave the charge of one to Christian, on whom Captain Bligh has always declared he had the greatest reliance. Such was his introduction to, and connection with, Captain Bligh; and every one must sincerely lament, that what in its commencement had been so honourable to both, should in its event and consequences have proved to both so disastrous and fatal.

The writer of this Appendix would think himself an accomplice in the crime which has been committed if he designedly should give the slightest shade to any word or fact different from its true and just representation; and lest he should be supposed to be actuated by a vindictive spirit, he has studiously forborn to make more comments than were absolutely necessary upon any statement which he has been obliged to bring forward. He has felt it a duty to himself, to the connections of all the unfortunate men, and to society, to collect and lay before the public these extraordinary circumstances.

The sufferings of Captain Bligh and his companions in the boat, however severe they may have been, are perhaps but a small portion of the torments occasioned by this dreadful event: and whilst these prove the melancholy and extensive consequences of the crime of mutiny, the crime itself in this instance may afford an awful lesson to the Navy, and to mankind, that there is a degree of pressure, beyond which the best formed and principled mind must either break or recoil. And though public justice and the public safety can allow no vindication of any species of mutiny, yet reason and humanity will distinguish the sudden unpremeditated act of desperation and frenzy, from the foul deliberate contempt of every religious duty and honourable sentiment; and will deplore the uncertainty of human prospects, when they reflect that a young man is condemned to perpetual infamy, who, if he had served on board any other ship, or had perhaps been absent from the *Bounty* a single day, or one ill-fated hour, might still have been an honour to his country, and a glory and comfort to his friends.

WILLIAM BLIGH'S ANSWER TO THE APPENDIX

An Answer to Certain Assertions Contained in the Appendix to a Pamphlet, Entitled:

Minutes of the Proceedings on the Court-Martial, held at Portsmouth, August 12th, 1792, on Ten Persons charged with Mutiny on Board His Majesty's Ship the Bounty

It is with no small degree of regret, that I find myself under the necessity of obtruding my private concerns on the Public. A pamphlet has appeared, under the title of *Minutes of the Proceedings on the Court-Martial, held at Portsmouth, August 12th, 1792, on Ten Persons charged with Mutiny on Board His Majesty's Ship the* Bounty; *with an Appendix, containing a full Account of the real Causes, &c. &c.* This Appendix is the work of Mr Edward Christian, the brother of Fletcher Christian, who headed the mutineers of the *Bounty*; written apparently for the purpose of vindicating his brother's conduct, at my expense.

The respect I owe to that public in whose service I have spent my life, as well as regard to my character, compel me to reply to such parts of Mr Christian's Appendix, as might, if unnoticed, obtain credit to my prejudice.

Of the Minutes of the Court-Martial, thus published, it is necessary to observe, that they differ from the Minutes lodged in the Admiralty-office; and in some places materially. One instance of this will appear among the Proofs, which are here submitted to the public.

The information which furnished Mr Edward Christian with materials for his Appendix, he states to 'have been collected from many interviews and conversations, in the presence and hearing of several respectable gentlemen.' He then mentions the names of all the persons with whom these conversations were held, without distinguishing the particular information given by any individual.

The mixing together the names of men, whose assertions merit very different degrees of credit, and blending their evidence into one mass, is liable to two objections: first the impossibility of tracing the author of any particular assertion; and secondly, the danger, which to a reader is unavoidable, of supposing, that the statements made by those who were actually accomplices in the mutiny, came from men of respectable character, with whom he has thus associated them.

One of the hardest cases which can befall any man is to be reduced to the necessity of defending his character by his own assertions only. As such, fortunately, is not my situation, I have rested my defence on the testimony of others; adding only, such of the written orders issued by me in the course of the voyage, as are connected with the matter in question; which orders being issued publicly in writing, may be offered as evidence of unquestionable credit.

These testimonials, without further remark from me, I trust, will be sufficient to do away any evil impression which the public may have imbibed, from reading Mr Edward Christian's defence of his brother.

LIST OF PROOFS

1. Orders issued upon our arrival at Otaheite, to regulate our intercourse with the Natives. October 25th, 1788.
2. Orders respecting the confinement of three men, who had deserted from the ship. January 24th, 1789.
3. Letter from the deserters beforementioned. January 26th, 1789.
4. Examination respecting the loss of His Majesty's Ship the *Bounty*, by the High Court of Judicature at Batavia. October 13th, 1789.
5. Descriptive list of the mutineers. 28th April, 1789.
6. Orders given to Mr John Fryer, the Master, on leaving him at Batavia. October 14th, 1789.
7. Letter from Mr Peter Haywood, Midshipman, to Mrs Bligh. July 14th, 1792.
8. Extract from Mr Peter Haywood's defence, on his trial by a court-martial; held August 12th, 1792, at Portsmouth.
9. Letter from Mr Peter Haywood to Mr Edward Christian, published in the *Cumberland Packet*, and *Whitehaven Advertiser*, November 20th, 1792.
10. Letter published in *The Times*, July 16th, 1794, from Mr Edward Harwood, late Surgeon of His Majesty's Ship *Providence*.
11. Affidavit of Joseph Coleman. July 31, 1794.
12. Affidavit of John Smith. August 1, 1794.

13. Affidavit of Lawrence Lebogue. August 2, 1794.

14. Letter from Lieutenant John Hallet. August 1,1794.

15. Letter from Mr Edward Lamb, Commander of the *Adventure*, in the Jamaica trade. October 28th, 1794.

No. 1.

Rules to be observed by every Person on Board, or belonging to the Bounty, *for the better establishing a trade for Supplies of Provisions, and good Intercourse with the Natives of the South Sea, wherever the Ship may be at.*

1st. At the Society, or Friendly Islands, no person whatever is to intimate that Captain Cook was killed by Indians; or that he is dead.

2nd. No person is ever to speak, or give the least hint, that we have come on purpose to get the breadfruit plant, until I have made my plan known to the chiefs.

3rd. Every person is to study to gain the good will and esteem of the natives; to treat them with all kindness; and not to take from them, by violent means, anything that they may have stolen; and no one is ever to fire, but in defence of his life.

4th. Every person employed on service, is to take care that no arms, or implements of any kind under their charge, are stolen; the value of such thing, being lost, shall be charged against their wages.

5th. No man is to embezzle, or offer to sale, directly, or indirectly, any part of the King's stores, of what nature soever.

6th. A proper person or persons will be appointed to regulate trade, and barter with the natives; and no officer or seaman, or other person belonging to the ship, is to trade for any kind of provisions, or curiosities; but if such officer or seaman wishes to purchase any particular thing, he is to apply to the provider to do it for him. By this means a regular market will be carried on, and all disputes, which otherwise may happen with the natives will be avoided. All boats are to have everything handed out of them at sunset.

Given under my hand, on board the *Bounty*,
Otaheite, 25th October, 1788.
Wm. Bligh

No. 2.
All prisoners are to be kept upon deck in fair weather; and the sentinel to report their state in the night, every half hour.

The key of their irons is to be taken care of by the master.

The mate of the watch is to be answerable for the prisoners. When they are released for a while, out of necessity, he is to see them again securely confined.

The mate of the watch is to have the charge of a brace of pistols, and one cartouche box, to be kept in the binnacle.

No canoe is to come on board after 8 o'clock at night, or any to go under the bows of the ship upon any pretence; but whatever is handed in or out of the ship is to be at the gangways.

All boats, when moored, to have everything handed out of them at sunset: and the sentinel is to report the state of the prisoners every half hour, after the watch is set.

Given under my hand, in Oparré harbour,
on board the *Bounty*, 24th January, 1789.
Wm. Bligh

No. 3.

Deserter's letter, dated on board the Bounty, *at Otaheite, 26th January, 1789.*

Sir,

We should think ourselves wholly inexhaustibility, if we omitted taking this earliest opportunity of returning our thanks for your goodness in delivering us from a trial by court-martial, the fatal consequences of which are obvious; and although we cannot possibly lay any claim to so great a favour, yet we humbly beg you will be pleased to remit any further punishment, and we trust our future conduct will fully demonstrate our deep sense of your clemency, and our steadfast resolution to behave better hereafter.

We are Sir,
Your most obedient, most humble servants,[1]
C Churchill,
Wm. Musprat,
John Millward

No. 4.

Translation of an examination before a Court of Inquiry, at Batavia, into the loss of the Bounty.

---

1 These three persons, who were afterwards mutineers, had run away with the large cutter, and a chest of firearms, and this is what Millward, on his trial by the court-martial, calls 'the former foolish affair.'

Oct 13, 1789

This day the 13th October, 1789, came before Nicholas Van Bergen Van der Gryp, notary public of the Noble High Regency of Netherland India, residing in the town of Batavia. Present, the hereafter to be named witnesses: John Fryer, master; Thomas Denman Ledward, surgeon; William Cole, boatswain; William Peckover, gunner; William Elphinston, master's mate; Thomas Hayward and John Hallet, midshipmen; John Samuel, secretary: and the sailors, Robert Tinkler, Peter Linkleter, Lawrence Lebogue, George Simpson, John Smith, and Robert Lamb; all here present declare, with previous knowledge of Mr Nicholas Englehard, superior Marchand, and Sabandhaar, and License Master in this place; and by interpretation of Mr Peter Aeneas Mackay, Sub Marchand, in the service of the Noble Company. That the truth is, they have been together, serving on board his Britannic Majesty's ship the *Bounty*, commanded by the Requirant.

Apr 28, 1789

That on the 28th April, 1789, that the greatest number of the ship's company, consisting of twenty-five persons, by the break of day, were mutineers; and before anybody had discovered or got notice of it, had already secured the requirant, binding his hands behind his back, and forcing him to come on deck in his shirt, where he was kept under a guard behind the mizen-mast. That the boatswain and the others were forced by the mutineers to assist in hoisting out the launch; which being done, they were forced to go into her, and the last of all the Requirant; after which they were veered astern of the ship by a rope, and soon after cast adrift in the wide ocean.

That they were in all nineteen souls in the launch, with a small quantity of bread and water, and no firearms.

That it had been impossible to foresee what has happened to them, as they had sailed homewards from the Friendly Islands, with a great cargo of plants, in the best order.

That there was no possibility to retake the ship, or do more for the welfare of the King's service, than what had been done by the Requirant, who had been tied and kept apart from the attestants until he was let down in the launch.

That there were heard at the time several expressions and huzzas in the ship, which makes them believe that the mutineers are returned to Otaheite.

Apr 28, 1789
May 2, 1789

That on the night of the 28th, they arrived at the island of Tofoa, one of the Friendly Islands, and remained there until the 2nd of May, 1789, seeking provisions and water. That they were attacked that day by the natives, whereby one man, John Norton, was killed, and they narrowly escaped.

Jun 14, 1789

That they, after having suffered all distress and misery, arrived the 14th June following at Coupang, in Timor, and that there David Nelson, gardener, died of a fever.

Aug 20, 1789
Oct 1, 1789
Oct 10, 1789

That they sailed from Coupang on the 20th August following in a schooner for that purpose purchased, and arrived here at

Batavia the 1st of October, 1789, where that vessel has been sold on the 10th of that month; that likewise on the 10th October died in the hospital, Thomas Hall.

Alleging that all abovementioned to be the truth and verity, offering to confirm this given attestation with solemn oath.

Thus acted and passed in presence of Hermanus Abraham Simonsz, and Francis Abraham Simonsz, clerks, as witnesses.

The minute of this act is in form signed, and put on stamp paper of 12 styvers.

Was signed N Bergen V D Gryp, Notary

Oct 15, 1789
This day, the 15th October, 1789, are heard by us, Gose Theodore Vermeer, and Jacobus Martinus Balze, Members in the Honourable Court of Eschevans Commissaries, being qualified thereto by that court, assisted by the sworn clerk, Johannis Lohr, all the above attestants named in this act, and under translation of the sworn translator in the English language, Louis Wybrand Van Schellebeck, on the repetition of this their deposition, in which they declare to persist, with demand only, that for more elucidation, the following changes may be made in it.

That the affair has happened in the vicinity of the Friendly Islands, near the island of Tofoa.

That the whole of the ship's company, at the time of the mutiny, consisted of forty-four persons, of which twenty-five have mutinied.

That, after they were overpowered, they heard the mutineers say, 'We shall in a short time return to the Society Islands'[1] and that the attestants, by homeward-bound, mean England.

On which, to prove the veracity of this their deposition, they give their oath, in the Protestant form.

Further is, by us Commissaries, in our qualifications, and on request of the Requirant, resolved of this act to give an account in forma dupla, of the same tenor and date, and both signed by the deposants, and authenticated by our common signature.

John Fryer,
T D Ledward,
Wm. Cole,
Wm. Peckover,
Wm. Elphinston,
Thos. Hayward,
John Hallet,
John Samuel,
Rob. Tinkler,
Peter Linkleter,
L Lebogue,
George Simpson,

---

1 This fact, and the huzzaing mentioned in the preceding page, are denied by Mr Edward Christian in a very pointed manner (see his Appendix); yet he professes to have received his information from 'every one of those who came in the boat', the very persons who had affirmed both circumstances on their oaths in this instrument.

John Smith,
Robt. Lamb

Signed by
G T Vermeer, J Balzee

Note. By desire of the Court I was not present at these examination. The originals are lodged in the Admiralty office.

No. 5.

Description of the pirates remaining on board His Majesty's armed vessel, Bounty, *on the 28th April, 1789. Drawn up at Timor, copies of this list were forwarded from Batavia to Lord Cornwallis, then Governor-General of India, at Calcutta; to Governor Philips, at New South Wales; and one was left at Batavia, with the Governor-General of the Dutch Possessions in India.*

Fletcher Christian, Master's Mate, aged 24 years, five feet nine inches high, blackish or very dark brown complexion, dark brown hair, strong made; a star tattooed on his left breast, tattooed on his backside; his knees stand a little out, and he may be called rather bow legged. He is subject to violent perspirations, and particularly in his hands, so that he soils anything he handles.

George Stewart, Midshipman, aged 24 years, five feet seven inches high, good complexion, dark hair, slender made, narrow chested, and long neck, small face, and black eyes; tattooed on the left breast with a star, and on the left arm with a heart and darts, is also tattooed on the backside.

Peter Haywood, Midshipman, aged 17 years, five feet seven inches high, fair complexion, light brown hair, well proportioned; very much tattooed; and on the right leg is tattooed the three legs of man, as it is upon that coin. At this time he has not done growing and speaks with the Manx, or Isle of Man accent.

Edward Young, Midshipman, aged 22 years, five feet eight inches high, dark complexion, and rather a bad look; dark brown hair, strong made, has lost several of his fore teeth, and those that remain are all rotten; a small mole on the left side of the throat, and on the right arm is tattooed a heart and dart through it, with EY underneath, and the date of the year 1788 or 1789.

Charles Churchill, Ship's Corporal, aged 30 years, five feet ten inches high, fair complexion, short light brown hair, top of the head bald, strong made; the forefinger of his left hand crooked, and his hand shews the marks of a sever scald; tattooed in several places of his body, legs, and arms.

James Morrison, Boatswain's Mate, aged 28 years, five feet eight inches high, sallow complexion, long black hair, slender made; has lost the use of the upper joint of the forefinger of the right hand; tattooed with a star under his left breast, and a garter round his left leg, with the motto of Honi soit qui mal y pense; and has been wounded in one of his arms with a musket ball.

John Mills, Gunner's Mate, aged 40 years, five feet ten inches high, fair complexion, light brown hair, strong made, and raw boned; a scar in his right armpit, occasioned by an abscess.

John Millward, Seaman, aged 22 years, five feet five inches high, brown complexion, dark hair, strong made; very much tattooed in different parts of the body, and under the pit of the stomach, with a taoomy of Otaheite.

Matthew Thompson, Seaman, aged 40 years, five feet eight inches high, very dark complexion, short black hair, slender made, and has lost the joint of the great toe of his right foot; and is tattooed in several places on his body.

William Mickoy, Seaman, aged 25 years, five feet six inches high, fair complexion, light brown hair, strong made; a scar where he has been stabbed in the belly, and a small scar under his chin; is tattooed in different parts of his body.

Matthew Quintal, Seaman, aged 21 years, five feet five inches high, fair complexion, light brown hair, strong made; very much tattooed on the backside, and several other places.

John Sumner, Seaman, aged 24 years, five feet eight inches high, fair complexion, brown hair; a scar on the left cheek, and tattooed in several places.

Thomas Burket, Seaman, aged 26 years, five feet nine inches high, fair complexion, very much pitted with the small-pox, brown hair, slender made, and very much tatowed.

Isaac Martin, Seaman, aged 30 years, five feet eleven inches high, sallow complexion, short brown hair, raw boned; tattooed with a star on his left breast.

William Musprat, Seaman, aged 30 years, five feet six inches high, dark complexion, brown hair, slender made, a very strong black beard, with scars under his chin; is tattooed in several places of his body.

Henry Hilbrant, Seaman, aged 25 years, five feet seven inches high, fair complexion, sandy hair, strong made; his left arm shorter than the other, having been broke; is an Hanoverian born, and speaks bad English; tattooed in several places.

Alexander Smith, Seaman, aged 22 years, five feet five inches high, brown complexion, brown hair, strong made; very much pitted with the smallpox, and very much tattooed on his body, legs, arms, and feet. He has a scar on his right foot, where it has been cut with a wood axe.

John Williams, Seaman, aged 25 years, five feet five inches high, dark complexion, black hair, slender made; has a scar on the back part of his head; is tattooed, and a native of Guernsey; speaks French.

Richard Skinner, Seaman, aged 22 years, five feet eight inches high, fair complexion, very well made, and has scars on both ankles, and on his right shin; is very much tattooed.

Thomas Ellison, Seaman, aged 17 years, five feet three inches high, fair complexion, dark hair, strong made; has got his name tattooed on his right arm, and dated October 25, 1788.

William Brown, Assistant Botanist, aged 27 years, five feet eight inches high, fair complexion, dark brown hair, slender made, a remarkable scar on one of his cheeks, which contracts the eyelid, and runs down to his throat, occasioned by the king's evil; is tattooed.

Michael Byrne, Seaman, aged 28 years, five feet six inches high, fair complexion, short fair hair, slender made: is almost blind, and has the mark of an issue on the back of his neck; plays the violin.

Joseph Coleman, Armourer, aged 40 years, five feet six inches high, fair complexion, grey hair, strong made; a heart tattooed on one of his arms.

Charles Norman, Carpenter's Mate, aged 26 years, five feet nine inches high, fair complexion, light brown hair, slender made, is pitted with the smallpox; and has a remarkable motion with his head and eyes.

Thomas McIntosh, Carpenter's Crew, aged 28 years, five feet six inches high, fair complexion, light brown hair, slender made; is pitted with the smallpox, and is tattooed.

The four last are deserving of mercy, being detained against their inclinations.

Wm. Bligh

Note. This description was made out from the recollections of the persons with me, who were best acquainted with their private marks.

No. 6.

Orders to Mr J Fryer, Master of the Bounty, *on my leaving him at Batavia.*

Oct 13, 1789
The board and lodging for yourself and Doctor, you may consider to be paid at one rix dollar per day; and for the boatswain, gunner, Mr Elphinston, Mr Hayward, and Mr Hallet, one rupee per day; and the charges for the seamen in the hospital, from the 13th October, you must pay as demanded, allowing for your brother, Robert Tinkler, at the same rate, to be put into the general account.

Should it be demanded of you to pay the passage money for every individual before you sail, you are to draw bills on the Treasurer of His Majesty's navy for the amount.

Before the ships are ready for sea, you are from time to time to apply to the Sabandhaar, Mr Englehard, who will assist you for the good of His Majesty's service; and through him, or as circumstances may point out, you are to make all necessary application to the Governor-General.

The remaining men and officers you are to take according to the ships they are put into, not separating Mr Hayward and Mr Hallet. The carpenter you must apply for to come with you, and is to be considered a prisoner at large in the ship.

On embarkation, you are to see that both officers and men conduct themselves with propriety and regularity.

On your arrival at the Cape of Good Hope, you are forthwith to join me; but should I not be there before the ship you sail in departs for Europe, you are to make the best of your way, in the same ship, and give an account of your transactions to the Admiralty.

While you remain here, you are to examine into the situation of the people in the hospital twice a week; and if they are not properly treated, you must represent the same to the Sabandhaar.

The carpenter having applied to me for clothes, you are to supply him with a month's pay to purchase the necessary articles he is in want of, and to see he is not ill-treated.

Given under my hand, at Batavia.
To Mr J Fryer, Master in His Majesty's navy.
Wm. Bligh

Oct 16, 1789
Whereas from a representation of the physician-general, it appears that my life is in great danger if I remain here until the fleet for Europe sails; and that only myself and two others can be taken in the packet, which departs on Friday the 16th instant;

I therefore empower you to take the command of the remaining officers and men, and order you to follow me to the Cape of Good Hope by the first ships His Excellency the Governor-General shall permit you to embark in; and as his Excellency has been pleased to order that the people may be taken care of at the convalescent hospital, about four miles from town, where is a good air and the best of treatment; you are hereby required to see that everyone remains there.

You are not to permit any of those who remain in town to be wandering about between the hours of nine in the morning and four in the afternoon.

You are, upon embarkation, or at a proper time, to get a knowledge of what charges are against His Majesty's subjects; and upon fairly and duly considering them, you are to draw bills for the amount on the Commissioners for victualling His Majesty's navy (if it cannot be done as hereafter expressed), giving them a letter of advice, at the same time, certifying that I sailed to the Cape of Good Hope before you, in a packet that could not take any more men; my health being so exceedingly impaired, as to render my existence very doubtful, and that the Governor-General could not give us all a passage in one ship.

I have agreed with the Sabandhaar that all debts of the government account, incurred for victualling or passage money, shall be presented to him; that then on your certifying the justness of it, and another signing officer, such account shall stand over until presented to government in England – that of all such accounts you are to secure copies, and to send them, by different opportunities, to me in England, signed as beforementioned, to the care of Messrs Marsh and Creed, agents, Norfolk-street, Strand. You are, for further security, to send one to your agent.

That before the departure of the people, you are to allow each seaman one month's pay to buy warm clothing to pass the Cape of Good Hope with, and you may also give the officers one month's pay for the same use, except yourself and Doctor.

I shall leave with you the money I received on the sale of the schooner – 177 ducatoons, or 295 rix dollars, for the expenditure of which you must produce regular vouchers; but you are to pay no account without consulting the Sabandhaar, that such account is at a moderate price.

No. 7.

His Majesty's Ship *Hector*, Portsmouth, July 14, 1792.

Dear Madam,

As I make no doubt you have already heard of my arrival here as a prisoner, to answer for my conduct done, on the day that unfortunate mutiny happened, which deprived Captain Bligh of his ship, and, I then feared, of life; but, thank God, it is otherwise: and I sincerely congratulate you, Madam, upon his safe, but miraculous, arrival in England; I hope, ere this, you have heard of the cause of my determination to remain in the ship; which being unknown to Captain Bligh, who unable to conjecture the reason, did, as I have had reason to fear, (I must say naturally) conclude, or rather suspect me to have likewise been a coadjutor in that unhappy affair; but God only knows, how little I merited so unjust a suspicion (if such a suspicion ever entered his breast); but yet my thorough consciousness of not having ever merited it, makes me sometimes flatter myself that he could scarcely be so cruel; and, ere long, let me hope I shall have an equitable tribunal to plead at; before which (through God's assistance) I shall have it in my power to proclaim my innocence, and clear up my long injured character before the world. I hear he is gone out again; if so, may he have all the success he can wish. Alas, Madam! I yesterday heard the melancholy news of the death of your best of parents; I heartily condole with you for his loss; for in him I lost the most kind friend and advocate; whose memory I shall for ever revere with the highest veneration.

I have one request to ask of you, Madam, which is, that you will be so obliging as to inquire whether Mrs Duncan, in Little Hermitage-street, hath in her possession the clothes (which, if you remember) I left with her in 1787, and gave you an order, by which you might at any time get them from her: so that if they are still there, you will be so good as to send them down here, directing them (for me, on board His Majesty's Ship *Hector*, to the care of Serjeant William Clayfield, marines, Portsmouth, or elsewhere): but if you can hear not tidings of them or her, you will honour with a few lines your much obliged,

obedient humble servant,

P Haywood

No. 8.

Extract from Mr P Haywood's defence, on his trial by a court-martial; held August 12th, 1792, at Portsmouth. Copied from the minutes of the court-martial, lodged in the Admiralty office[1].

---

1 This part of Mr Haywood's defence does not appear in the Minutes of the court-martial published, or in Mr Edward Christian's Appendix.

'Captain Bligh, in his Narrative, acknowledges that he had left some friends on board the *Bounty*; and no part of my conduct could have induced him to believe that I ought not to be reckoned of the number. Indeed, from his attention to, and very kind treatment of me personally, I should have been a monster of depravity to have betrayed him. The idea alone is sufficient to disturb a mind, where humanity and gratitude have, I hope, ever been noticed as its characteristic features.'

No. 9.

The following letter, signed P Haywood, with the remarks, appeared in the Cumberland Packet, *or* Ware's Whitehaven Advertiser, *November 20th, 1792, about three months after the court-martial.*

The late most interesting trial at Portsmouth, of the unfortunate mutineers of the *Bounty*, will be shortly published by a gentleman of respectability, who was employed before the court-martial. That publication will astonish the world; and the public will then correct the erroneous opinions, which, from certain false narratives, they have long entertained; and will be enabled to distinguish between the audacious and hardened depravity of the heart, which no suffering can soften, and the desperation of an ingenuous mind, torn and agonised by unprovoked and incessant abuse and disgrace.

Though there may be certain actions, which even the torture and extremity of provocation cannot justify, yet a sudden act of frenzy, so circumstanced, is far removed, in reason and mercy, from the foul, deliberate contempt of every religious and

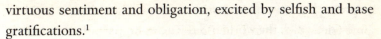

virtuous sentiment and obligation, excited by selfish and base gratifications.[1]

For the honour of this country, we are happy to assure our readers that one of its natives, Fletcher Christian, is not that detestable and horrid monster of wickedness, which with extreme, and perhaps unexampled, injustice and barbarity to him and his relations, he has long been represented: but a character for whom every feeling heart must now sincerely grieve and lament.

When Mr Haywood, the midshipman, had received His Majesty's free pardon, he felt it his duty to write to Mr Christian's brother the following letter:

Great Russell-Street, 5 Nov 1792

Sir,

I am sorry to say, I have been informed you were inclined to judge too harshly of your truly unfortunate brother; and to think of him in such a manner, as I am conscious, from the knowledge I had of his most worthy disposition and character (both public and private), he merits not, in the slightest degree: therefore I think it my duty to undeceive you, and to rekindle the flame of brotherly love (or pity now) towards him, which I fear the false reports of slander, and vile suspicion, may have nearly extinguished.

Excuse my freedom, sir: if it would not be disagreeable to you, I will do myself the pleasure of waiting upon you, and endeavour

---

1 The great resemblance between the last page of Mr Edward Christian's Appendix and this paragraph is very remarkable, if they were written by different persons.

to prove that your brother was not that vile wretch, void of all gratitude, which the world had the unkindness to think him: but, on the contrary, a most worthy character; ruined only by having the misfortune, if it can be so called, of being a young man of strict honour, and adorned with every virtue; and beloved by all (except one, whose ill report is his greatest praise) who had the pleasure of his acquaintance.

I am, sir, with esteem,
Your most obedient humble servant,
P Haywood

This character, every officer and seaman, except one, on board the *Bounty*, who has yet arrived in England, now unites in bestowing upon him. The mystery of this transaction will soon be unravelled, and then the shame and infamy of it will be distributed, in the just proportions in which they are, and have been, deserved.

No. 10.
Taken from The Times, *July 16th, 1794*
To the Conductor of The Times

Sir,
A publication has lately made it appearance, entitled, *Minutes of the Proceedings of the Court-Martial, held at Portsmouth August 12th, 1792, on Ten Persons charged with Mutiny on Board His Majesty's Ship* Bounty; *with an Appendix, containing a full Account of the real Causes and Circumstances of that unhappy Transaction, the most material of which have hitherto been withheld from the*

Public; written by Edward Christian. The obvious tendency of which is to palliate the conduct of Fletcher Christian, his brother, and ultimately to asperse the character of Captain Bligh. As if anything could be advanced in extenuation of a crime, at the bare recital of which humanity shudders; a crime, marked by such circumstances as to be unexampled in the annals of nautical history. This publication, Mr Editor, is disgraced by gross misrepresentations, and low malevolence, of which innumerable instances could be adduced, were long details admissible in a newspaper. The shafts of envy are ever levelled against conspicuous merit, but they recoil with redoubled force on the impotent adversary. Captain Bligh's general conduct during the late expedition, which was crowned with the most ample success, his affability to his officers, and humane attention to his men, gained him their high esteem and admiration, and must eventually dissipate any unfavourable opinion, hastily adopted in his absence. I trust that this imbecile and highly illiberal attack, directed by the brother of the arch-mutineer, will be received by the world with that indignation and contempt it so justly deserves.

I remain, sir, your humble servant,
Ed Harwood,
Late Surgeon of His Majesty's Ship *Providence*

No. 11.
Affidavit of Joseph Coleman

I Joseph Coleman, late belonging to His Majesty's armed vessel *Bounty*, William Bligh, Esq. Commander, voluntarily do make oath,

That Mr Edward Christian sent for me, and asked me concerning the mutiny in the *Bounty*, and about Captain Bligh; and I said, I knew nothing of him, but that he was a very good man to me.

I told Mr Christian, that [I] never heard Captain Bligh say, he would make his officers jump overboard, and eat grass like cows.

I told him, that after the ship was taken, I heard the mutineers say, he swore and damned them; but not that I heard him do it myself. I said, I could never agree with the mutineers.

I never saw Captain Bligh shake his hand in Christian's face or heard him damn him for not firing at the Indians.

I do not remember any thing about the heap of coconuts being taken away, but by hearsay from the mutineers, after the ship was taken, and we came home.

I never heard, or told Mr Edward Christian, about his brother's expression, that 'he had been in hell for weeks past with you.'

I never knew or heard that Captain Bligh and Fletcher Christian had any words at the Cape, or before the mutiny.

I never told, or heard, of Captain Bligh telling the chiefs at Otaheite, that Christian was a towtow (or servant).

I never knew anything of Christian intending to make a raft, to quit the ship.

I never told Mr Christian that Stewart clapped his hands, and said, it was the happiest day of his life.

I remember Christian having a girl, and of her going with him to the island Tobooy, and lived with him.

I said, I never could be easy with the mutineers, because they knew I was kept against my will. Morrison threatened to blow my brains out.

I remember that Musprat, Churchill, and Millward, deserted with the cutter and arms, while at Otaheite, and that they said many others intended to remain among the islands.

I remember that one of our cables was almost cut through at Otaheite, and that afterwards the Captain had always a sentinel on the bowsprit.

I know the Captain never suffered any man to hurt the Indians, or insult them.

I know we were at short allowance of bread, and that we were at two-thirds allowance of that article; but I remember, that by the consent of everyone, we had only grog every other day while at Otaheite, and that was, that we might not be in want in case we cold not get through Endeavour Straits, and we did not want it so much at Otaheite, because we had plenty of coconut milk.

I never said more to Mr Christian, than that his brother behaved very well to me after the mutiny, and that I knew no harm of him before the mutiny.

I never said, that Christian, or Stewart, was equal to Captain Bligh in abilities, I never thought of such a thing.

Joseph Coleman,
Sworn before me, at the Public Office in Great Marlborough-street, this 31st day of July, 1794. Signed John Scott

No. 12.
John Smith's Affidavit.

I John Smith late belonging to His Majesty's armed vessel the *Bounty*, William Bligh, Esq. Commander, maketh oath, that Mr

Edward Christian sent for me, and asked me how his brother (who was the mutineer in the *Bounty*) had behaved in the ship.

I said his brother was well liked in the ship, as far as I knew, by the people.

I never knew Christian and Captain Bligh have any words particular.

On the day before the mutiny happened, I was sent by the Captain to ask Christian to dine with him; but he said, I am so ill I cannot wait on the Captain: and I was sent again in the evening to ask Christian to supper, and he said he was so ill that he could not come.

When in working the ship, and things had been neglected to have been done at other times that the Captain had ordered, I have known the Captain to be angry and damn the people, as is common; but the Captain immediately afterwards always behaved to the people as if nothing had happened.

I never heard the Captain damn the officers, and call them names, and threaten to make them jump overboard, kill half of them, and make them eat grass like cows. I never heard any such a thing.

I never saw the Captain shake his hand in Christian's face, and I never heard of it even that he did; or in any of their faces.

I never heard that the Captain damned Christian for not firing at the Indians for stealing an adze.

I did not hear Christian say to the Captain, I am in hell I am in hell, because I was below; but I never understood but that he did say so. The Captain said so in the boat, and had it in his Narrative, which I never heard anyone deny.

I never told Mr Edward Christian any thing about the coconuts, or did I know anything about it, any more than that the Captain found fault at a heap of coconuts being taken away; and I never knew or heard that such a thing could be the cause of the mutiny.

I never knew or heard of any words that the Captain had with Christian at the Cape of Good Hope; but I always understood he was on good terms with the Captain, and remember he used to dine with him every third day, and did so until the day of the mutiny, and frequently supped with the Captain besides.

I never heard, or told Mr Edward Christian, that Captain Bligh told the people of Otaheite, that his brother was a towtow (or servant), or ever heard of such a thing.

I never knew anything that Christian intended to make a raft, or ever heard of it until the Mutineers arrived in the *Pandora*, and I never told Mr Edward Christian about it.

I never told Mr Edward Christian that his brother, or Stewart, was equal to Captain Bligh in abilities, nobody could say such a thing as that – I always saw Captain Bligh instructing him.

I never said to Mr Edward Christian anything about his brother's abilities, or anything respecting his qualifications, or the praises which he, in his Appendix, says were repeated by one and the other.

I remember that Christian always had leave to have grog out of Captain Bligh's case whenever he wanted it; and I always gave it him, and Mr Nelson the gardener, when they chose to ask for it.

I know that we were never at short allowance of provisions except bread, and that was one-third short; but I remember that at Otaheite, all hands, by their own consent, had their grog but every other day, on account of the danger of going through Endeavour Straits, where we might lose our passage; and the want of grog at Otaheite we did not mind, because we had plenty of fine coconut milk, and the finest fresh pork, breadfruit, and other things of the country.

Mr Edward Christian asked me how Captain Bligh was liked in the *Providence*, and if nothing had happened, and I told him nothing had happened, and all was well, and the Captain very much liked.

I know the Captain was always very kind to the Indians, and would not suffer any man to hurt or insult them.

This is all that I said to Mr Christian, the brother of Christian the mutineer on board the *Bounty*; and Mr Christian had no right to make use of my name in the manner he has done in his first publication.

I know that three of the mutineers, Musprat, Churchill, and Millward, while at Otaheite, ran away with the cutter and arms.

I remember our cable being cut nearly through at Otaheite, in a stormy night, and that Captain Bligh afterwards ordered a sentinel on the bowsprit.

John Smith
Sworn before me at Guildhall, London, this 1st August, 1794.
Signed Watkin Lewes

No. 13.
Lawrence Lebogue's Affidavit.

I Lawrence Lebogue, late sailmaker on board His Majesty's armed vessel *Bounty*, William Bligh, Esq. Commander, do voluntarily make oath.

That I was sent for by Mr Edward Christian to a public-house, and asked whether Captain Bligh did flog his people, and why he kept them at short allowance; but the most of his questions were about Captain Bligh's behaviour to the officers of the *Providence*, and how he behaved to them, and if I thought they liked him.

I told him that Captain Bligh made no distinction, every officer was obliged to do his duty, and he showed no more favour to one man than another. I was sure every person in the *Providence* would speak well of Captain Bligh – he was a father to every person.

I said I knew Captain Bligh was a very great friend to Christian the mutineer; he was always permitted to use the Captain's cabin, where I have seen the Captain teaching him navigation and drawing. He was permitted to use the Captain's liquor when he wanted it, and I have many times gone down at night to get him grog out of the Captain's case.

I have heard the Captain damn the people, like many other captains; but he was never angry with a man the next minute; and I never heard of their disliking him.

I never heard of the Captain abusing his officers; nor ever said to Mr Edward Christian that he threatened to make them jump overboard; or eat grass like cows; or shake his hand in their faces.

I said, Captain Bligh was not a person fond of flogging his men; and some of them deserved hanging, who had only a dozen.

I said we were never at short allowance but in bread, and that we were at two-thirds, because we did not know how long it would be before we got a supply, as we had to go through a terrible passage near new Guinea. And for fear of being in want of spirits, the ship's company had agreed, while at Otaheite, to have their grog but every other day, because they had plenty of fine coconut milk, and all they cared about.

I remember that a heap of coconuts, which the Captain had ordered to be saved as a rarity until we got to sea, for a day or two, when we should enjoy them, was taken away; and that the Captain told the officers they had neglected their duty, and disobeyed his orders; and that all the coconuts, on that account, were brought upon deck; and the matter ended with their being divided.

I never heard nor told Mr Edward Christian anything about – I have been in hell, which he speaks of.

I never knew, or heard, that Christian was ever found fault with by Captain Bligh at the Cape of Good Hope; and I always thought they were very friends, until the mutiny.

I remember very well that the Captain came on deck one night and found fault with Christian, because in a squall he had not taken care of the sails. It was after we left Whytootackee.[1]

I never knew that Christian intended to go away on a raft; or could he have made one without its being known by every person.

I remember Christian had a girl, who was always with him.

I never heard anything at Otaheite that Captain Bligh had told the chiefs, Christian was a towtow; I know the chiefs did not think so of any of the officers.

I never knew Captain Bligh find fault with Christian for not firing at the Indians at Anamoka.

I was the only person mentioned who sailed with Captain Bligh to the West Indies, and to the South Sea, as Christian did; and I never told Mr Edward Christian that his brother could not have borne Captain Bligh's conduct to him much longer, because I knew Captain Bligh was always a friend to Christian, when he sailed with him to the West Indies, as well as afterwards.

I know that three of the mutineers deserted with one of the boats and an arm chest with arms at Otaheite, because they

---

1 Mr Edward Christian declares no one ever knew of this circumstance.

wished to stay among the islands. Musprat, Churchill, and Millward were the three, and they said many others intended to do it.

I remember one of our cables being almost cut through in a dark stormy night, which we thought was to let the ship go on shore; and that after that, the Captain ordered a sentinel on the bowsprit. This was at Otaheite.

Mr Christian asked me if I thought Captain Bligh could hurt his brother, if he ever came home. I said Captain Bligh had such a forgiving temper that I did not think he would, unless the law of his country would hurt him. I said Captain Bligh was the best friend Christian ever had.

I remember that Christian was drinking with the carpenter, William Purcell, at 12 o'clock at night, although Christian was to be up at 4 o'clock in the morning to keep his watch, and that when the mutiny broke out that morning, I saw a musket at Purcell, the carpenter's cabin door.

Lawrence Lebogue
Sworn to the truth of the foregoing Narrative
2nd day August, 1794, at Guildhall, London
Signed Watkin Lewes

No. 14.
From Lieutenant John Hallet to Captain Bligh.

Dear Sir,
I have just read a publication, by Mr Edward Christian, respecting the mutiny on board the *Bounty*, and have made a few

remarks thereon, which I have transmitted to you, and beg that you will make any use of them you please.

I am, dear sir,
Your obedient humble, servant,
John Hallet, Junior

Having been long confined by a severe illness, and having consequently not mixed with the world since my arrival, in February last, from Jamaica; it was but lately that the minutes of the court-martial, held in 1792, on ten persons charged with mutiny on board the *Bounty*; together with an Appendix to those minutes, published by Mr Edward Christian, reached my hands. As I was on board the *Bounty* at the time of the mutiny, and as my name is not wholly unimplicated in the Appendix, I cannot but consider myself bound, in justice to my own character, as well as to that of Captain Bligh, to advance my mite towards the confutation of the very malevolent assertions and insinuations conveyed to the public through the medium of that Appendix. I will by no means affirm that I never heard Captain Bligh express himself in warm or hasty language, when the conduct of his officers or people has displeased him; but every seafaring gentleman must be convinced that situations frequently occur in a ship when the most mild officer will be driven, by the circumstances of the moment, to utter expressions which the strict standard of politeness will not warrant: and I can safely assert that I never remember to have heard Captain Bligh make use of such illiberal epithets and menaces as the Appendix attributes to him. I must likewise declare that I always considered Captain Bligh as being a friend to Christian; and I have frequently heard Fletcher Christian assert that he had conducted himself as such. I remember a complaint of some coconuts having been stolen, but I did not hear that Captain Bligh accused any individual of the theft.

As to the insinuation of the people being at short allowance of provisions, I remember being at two-thirds allowance of bread; but at and from Otaheite, there was full allowance, and fresh pork was thrown overboard, because it could not be eaten while it was good; and during our stay there, we were at half allowance of grog. Whether the mutiny was preconcerted or not, is a question which can be solved only by those who were concerned in it; because any officer or man apprised of the circumstances, and not being a party in it, must have been compelled, if not by his duty, at least by the desire of self-preservation, to have counteracted the plot by his information and exertions.

Much stress is laid on the most part having gone voluntarily into the boat; in answer to which, I would only ask any person, endued with a proper sense of honour, if he would not rather commit himself to the evident danger of the boat, than incur the risk of an ignominious death, or the stigma of being arraigned as a pirate?

The Appendix charges Mr Hayward and myself with the imputation of being asleep in our watch. With regard to myself, I deny the accusation; and with regard to Mr Hayward (who is now absent on service), I have reason to believe it is equally false, as I had conversed with him a few minutes before. Besides what immediately belonged to Captain Bligh, every person in the boat had some useful articles; and many general necessaries were included.

I am likewise accused of uttering some dissatisfaction to Captain Bligh in the boat, to which Mr Edward Christian seems desirous of attaching much criminality. I can only say that I do not remember to have used such words imputed to me; and even if I had uttered them, they are such as would bear an interpretation diametrically opposite to that put upon them. And it is worthy of observation, that by the kind addition of a note, my whole offence is concentered in the innocent word resource.

As to Mr Christian's ability as an artist, or a seaman, I never considered them to bear any competition with those of Captain Bligh: and he certainly could not be called a fine scholar; as he did not appear to have received any portion of classical education, and was ignorant of all but his native language.

My situation in the *Bounty*, together with a proper regard to truth, and the introduction of my name in the Appendix, has compelled me to advance so much, uninfluenced by any personal animosity to Mr Fletcher Christian, whose memory I wish had been quietly committed to oblivion; as I am convinced that the stain will be deeper impressed on his name, by the endeavours which his friends have exerted in vindication of his character.

John Hallet Junior
Manchester Buildings,
1st Aug, 1794

No. 15.
Letter from Mr Edward Lamb, Commander of the Adventure, *in the Jamaica Trade, to Captain Bligh.*

St George's Place, St George's in the East,
Oct 28, 1794

Dear Sir,

Upon my arrival from Jamaica, I saw a pamphlet, published by Mr Edward Christian, who, in order to lessen the guilt of his brother, Mr Fletcher Christian, wishes to make the public believe that the mutiny on board His Majesty's Ship the *Bounty*, proceeded from your treatment of his brother, and the other mutineers. I was much surprised at what Mr Edward Christian has introduced in the Appendix, as he insinuates that your bad behaviour to Mr Fletcher Christian commenced during his last voyage with you to Jamaica, in the ship *Britannia*, when I was chief mate, and eyewitness to every thing that passed. Mr Edward Christian must have been misinformed, and known very little either of his brother's situation, abilities, or the manner in which he conducted himself during that voyage, he mentions his being second mate with you, when, in fact, he was no officer. I recollect your putting him upon the articles as gunner, telling me, at the same time, you wished him to be thought an officer; and desired I would endeavour to make the people look upon him as such.

When we got to sea, and I saw your partiality for the young man, I gave him every advice and information in my power, though he went about every point of duty with a degree of indifference, that to me was truly unpleasant; but you were blind to his faults, and had him to dine and sup every other day in the cabin, and treated him like a brother, in giving him every information. In the Appendix it is said, that Mr Fletcher Christian had no attachment amongst the women at Otaheite; if that was the case, he must have been much altered since he was with you in the *Britannia*; he was then one of the most foolish young men I ever knew in regard to the sex. You will excuse the liberty I have taken in addressing you upon so unpleasant a subject; but I could not pass over many assertions in the Appendix without feeling for a man whose kind and uniform behaviour to me, through the whole voyage to Jamaica, was such as to lay me under an everlasting obligation; and I shall still think myself fortunate in having engaged with such an attentive officer, and able navigator as yourself.

I have no pique at Mr Fletcher Christian; but finding Captain Bligh's character suffering in the opinion of the public, I think it my duty to offer my services in the vindication of it, so far as comes within my knowledge; therefore, can I render him any service, he may command me.

I remain, sir,
Your most obliged and humble servant,
Edward Lamb

Conclusion

I submit these evidences to the judgment of the public, without offering any comment. My only intention in this publication is to clear my character from the effect of censures which I am conscious I have not merited: I have therefore avoided troubling the public with more than what is necessary to that end; and have refrained from remark, lest I might have been led beyond my purpose, which I have wished to limit solely to defence.

William Bligh
3rd Dec, 1794

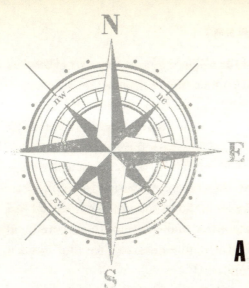

A SHORT REPLY

Edward Christian's Reply to William Bligh's Answer to the Appendix

If Captain William Bligh's Answer had been confined to endeavours to refute the imputations upon his conduct, contained in the minutes of the proceedings of the court-martial, or in the Appendix annexed to it, I should have been glad to have left him in possession of any benefit or success which those endeavours might have been attended with. But as almost all the material parts of what are called proofs are little more than insinuations that the statements, which I thought it my duty to lay before the public, have been unfairly obtained, or unfairly represented, I feel myself called upon to make a few observations in vindication of my own conduct and character. The first intimation which I received, that the dreadful mutiny on board the *Bounty* originated from motives, and was attended with circumstances, different from those which had been represented to the world,

MUTINY ON BOARD HMS BOUNTY

was in consequence of the following letter from Mr Haywood, and which is printed in Captain Bligh's Answer.

Great Russell-Street, 5th Nov 1792

Sir,

I am sorry to say, I have been informed you were inclined to judge too harshly of your truly unfortunate brother; and to think of him in such a manner as I am conscious, from the knowledge I had of his most worthy disposition and character (both public and private) he merits not in the slightest degree: therefore I think it my duty to undeceive you, and to rekindle the flame of brotherly love (or pity now) towards him, which, I fear, the false reports of slander and vile suspicion may have nearly extinguished.

Excuse my freedom, sir: if it would not be disagreeable to you, I will do myself the pleasure of waiting upon you; and endeavour to prove that your brother was not that vile wretch, void of all gratitude, which the world had the unkindness to think him; but, on the contrary, a most worthy character, ruined only by having the misfortune (if it can be so called) of being a young man of strict honour, and adorned with every virtue; and beloved by all (except one, whose ill report is his greatest praise) who had the pleasure of his acquaintance.

I am, sir, with esteem,
Your most obedient humble servant,
P Haywood

Having had an interview with Mr Haywood, I immediately communicated the information I had received to a confidential friend of mine, Mr Romilly, a barrister of Lincoln's Inn; and, by his advice, I afterwards waited upon a gentleman, then high in the profession of the law, who has since been advanced to the bench, and who now presides in one of the courts in Westminster-hall. The object of that visit was to inquire of him what credit was due to the account I had heard, as it had been mentioned in the newspapers that he was present at the trial. His Lordship received me with that politeness and benevolence which have ever distinguished his character. It might be thought indelicate in me to relate any conversation that passed between his Lordship and me; and I trust he will have the goodness to forgive the liberty I have taken in referring to this interview with his Lordship, as a strong proof of the caution with which I wished to proceed in this inquiry.

Although it is true that I received the first intimation of the circumstances related in the Appendix from Mr Haywood, yet, before I saw that gentleman, Mr Fryer (the master of the *Bounty*) had communicated the same circumstances to Mr Joseph Christian of the Strand, No 10, which were made known to me soon after the conversation I had with Mr Haywood. He is a distant relation of mine; his name had induced Mr Fryer to call upon him, and give him the information. From that time I was determined to investigate the subject fully; and I had the precaution upon every occasion (except when I called upon Mr Hayward of Hackney) when I expected to see any of the people of the *Bounty* to have some gentlemen in company with me. By the favour of these gentlemen I have published their names and places of residence that any person interested in the subject might have an opportunity of making inquiries of them whether the information I received in their company has or has not been fairly represented by me.

It is unnecessary for me to declare that the list is filled with the names of gentlemen who may be justly said to be the most honourable characters in society; and I may be truly proud in calling them my friends. If I could have entertained a thought of misrepresenting the testimony, to the prejudice of Captain Bligh, I ought to be considered the most infamous of mankind; and if in fact I have misrepresented it, I must have forfeited the esteem of the most valuable part of my acquaintance, and must have incurred a punishment almost equivalent to banishment from society. But I still hope that I shall continue, whilst I live, to enjoy their good opinion and their friendship.

Captain Bligh has published Mr Haywood's letter as one of his proofs. I presume, with intent to prove the inconsistency between that letter and a passage taken from Mr Haywood's defence, in which he speaks strongly of Captain Bligh's attention and kind treatment to him personally. A note is subjoined, that 'this part of Mr Haywood's defence does not appear in the minutes of the court-martial published, or in Mr Edward Christian's Appendix.' As far as this is an insinuation of a wilful omission on my part, I need only answer that Mr Barney has declared, in his prefatory letter, that his minutes did not extend beyond the evidence for the prosecution. This passage was therefore not contained in those minutes, nor was it in any copy which I could command. I anxiously solicited (as all my friends know) another gentleman to publish, or to permit me to publish, his copy of the minutes, which contained the several defences of the prisoners. Being unable to prevail upon him, I waited upon one of the Lords of the Admiralty to request the copy transmitted to the board. He politely informed me that it could not be granted to any individual in a private situation. I shall therefore, I trust, stand acquitted of any imputation of having industriously suppressed this testimonial in Captain Bligh's favour.

It may be also observed that Mr Haywood's letter complains of no ill treatment received by him personally from Captain Bligh, and that the defence was drawn up by his counsel when he was tried for his life, charged with an act which can admit of no justification; and I have the authority of one of his counsel to declare that his defence was left entirely to their discretion. Captain Bligh has inserted among his proofs, a letter signed by Ed. Harwood, late surgeon of his Majesty's Ship *Providence*. This letter is a certificate by the surgeon, and by the surgeon only, of Captain Bligh's good conduct in the *Providence*; but, as Mr Harwood never belonged to the *Bounty*, it is difficult to say how it can be considered as a proof of any circumstance which ever occurred on board that ship. Indeed, if abuse and scurrility can be regarded as evidence, it is true that no proof can be stronger. When it was published in the newspaper *The Times*, I was advised to treat it with silent contempt; and I should have thought myself degraded in the opinion of every man of sense and honour if I had condescended to have taken notice of so illiberal and indecent a letter.

With regard to the affidavits made by Joseph Coleman, who is a pensioner in Chelsea Hospital, and by John Smith, who was Captain Bligh's servant, and I am told is now living in his house, I have not much to object to them. Most of the paragraphs begin with 'I never told Mr Ed. Christian, etc' These two persons might easily be induced, without much (or any) violence to their consciences, to swear thus in negatives. Coleman has the appearance of a decent and honest man, but he is old and dull; and I never saw him but in the company of other persons belonging to the *Bounty*, who took the lead in conversation; but to their information he certainly in every instance assented by his silence, or without making any contradiction. The only observation I ever remember him to have made was, that 'Mr Christian was a fine young man, or a fine young officer'; and throughout the whole of the Appendix there is not a single word used by me as referable to his evidence. John Smith, the Captain's servant, I never saw but once: he came of his own accord to my chambers. He spoke of Mr Christian in the highest terms of praise and affection; and the sentence in the Appendix was spoken by him, viz 'Mr Christian was always good-natured; I never heard him say Damn you to any man on board the ship.' He said, that 'during the mutiny he ran backward and forward to put all the Captain's things on board the launch; that he was not ordered to leave the ship, but that he went of his own accord, thinking it his duty to follow his master: that there was no huzzaing on board.'

Being then asked what could be the cause of the mutiny, and if there had been any previous misunderstanding between Christian and the Captain; he said he could not speak to that, as his duty as cook and Captain's servant confined him below, and he could not say what might have passed upon deck. I told him he spoke like an honest man, and that I should not trouble him with any more questions. It was very fortunate that Mr Gilpin in the Strand, No 432, happened to be in my chambers at the time. Mr Gilpin had an opportunity of seeing several more persons belonging to the *Bounty*. He can bear witness that this man's information was perfectly consistent, as far as it went, with the account which he heard from the others. Mr Gilpin, and every gentleman whose name I have used, I am confident will always do me the justice to declare that what they have heard I have represented fairly, and without the slightest exaggeration. I may add too, that they have all a numerous and honourable acquaintance, who must be perfectly convinced that they would each of them reprobate, with an honest indignation, an attempt to give authenticity by their names to a statement which was inconsistent with their notions of the purest honour and the strictest justice; and which at the same time must necessarily wound the feelings or lessen the reputation of any individual.

Though I have said I have little objection to make to the two first affidavits, yet I am obliged to declare that the third, which is made by Lawrence Lebogue, is the most wicked and perjured affidavit that ever was sworn before a magistrate, or published to the world; and it is perhaps a defect in the law that these voluntary affidavits are permitted to be made; or that, when they are false, the authors of them are subject to no punishment. For if Lawrence Lebogue had made the same affidavit in a court of justice, he would most probably, upon the united evidence of three gentlemen, have been convicted of the grossest and foulest perjury. John Atkinson, Esq. Somerset Heraid, and James Losh, Esq. Barrister of the Temple, went with me to dine at the Crown and Sceptre at Greenwich. After dinner we sent to the hospital for Joseph Coleman, Michael Byrne, and Lawrence Lebogue, three of the pensioners who had belonged to the *Bounty*. Coleman and Byrne were at home, and came immediately; Lebogue could not then be found. After much conversation with Coleman and Byrne, in which Byrne took the lead, Lebogue came into the room; and without any hesitation (at which we were much surprised, as he had sailed a second time with Captain Bligh in the *Providence*), he gave a full detail, in clear and strong language, of all the material circumstances recited in the Appendix, and which we had just before heard from Byrne.

Mr Atkinson and Mr Losh have given me permission to publish the following certificate from them:

'We were present with Mr Edward Christian at the Crown and Sceptre at Greenwich, and had much conversation with Michael Byrne. Joseph Coleman, and Lawrence Lebogue, and upon another day a long conversation with Mr Peckover, respecting the unfortunate mutiny on board the *Bounty*; in which conversations we observed no contradiction or inconsistency: and we hereby declare that we think that the result of these conversations is faithfully and without exaggeration represented by Mr Edward Christian, in the Appendix to the minutes of the court-martial: and we also declare that we were much astonished at reading Lebogue's affidavit in Captain Bligh's Answer; as we believe that all the material paragraphs in that affidavit respecting the conversation we had with him at Greenwich are directly the reverse of the truth; and this we should be ready to make oath of, if it were necessary. We also declare that Mr Peckover asserted in our company that he was upon shore with Mr Christian all the time the ship was at Otaheite, and that Mr Christian had no favourite or particular connection among the women.'

John Atkinson, Heralds' College
James Losh, Temple

Some of the questions, indeed, attributed to me in that affidavit, must have proceeded from such extreme weakness and folly, that I cannot but flatter myself that those who know me will think that they carry with them internal evidence of misrepresentation. Though this man has not only retracted all that he told us, but has had the audacity to swear to the direct contrary, I shall appeal to every candid reader which are most to be credited – his simple declarations made without any solicitation, and which corresponded with the accounts given by several others at different times; or an affidavit made to serve his captain, directly the reverse of what he himself declared, and an affidavit for which in this world he is subject to no punishment whatever.

As to Mr Hallet's letter to Captain Bligh, I have only to observe upon it that Mr Hallet was not in England before the Appendix was published, and this letter is now published after his death. If I had had an opportunity of seeing Mr Hallet, I certainly should have thought myself much obliged to him if he would have corrected any misrepresentation which I had received from others. But he certainly is mistaken when he thinks so unkindly of me as to suppose I meant any malevolent or false accusations against him.

Nor would it, I conceive, have been a very heinous offence, if what I had been told was true, that two young men, viz himself and Mr Hayward then about 15 or 16 years of age, had fallen asleep in their watch after 4 o'clock in the morning: and if the mutiny had not been preconcerted (and Mr Hallet himself admits there was no proof that it was so) and if these two young gentlemen were not asleep, it will appear to have been more sudden in its commencement, as it must have been proposed and resolved upon whilst they were upon deck, but out of hearing.

I am sorry that Mr Hallet has ventured to assert that 'Christian did not appear to have received any portion of classical learning, and was ignorant of all but his mother tongue.' It is very probable that a young midshipman may be unacquainted with the extent of the learning of any other officer on board; but Mr Hallet's assertion that Christian was absolutely ignorant has been made either with too little caution or too much zeal. Christian was educated by the Reverend Mr Scott, at St Bees school in Cumberland, where the young men of the best families in that country receive their education, and from which many are sent to the universities; and I am confident that Mr Scott, his school-fellows, and all who knew him well, will testify that 'Christian was an excellent scholar, and possessed extraordinary abilities.' This is a point which a great number of gentlemen in the most respectable situations in life must be acquainted with; and I shall leave it to them to determine, whether Mr Hallet or I, in this instance, be most deserving of credit.

I was sorry also to see in the letter written by Mr Lamb, who had once been a mate to Captain Bligh in the merchant's service, an attempt to degrade Christian's character, by stating, that he went about every point of duty with a degree of indifference, that to him (Mr Lamb) was truly unpleasant. This representation is certainly different from the character which Captain Bligh himself has always given of Christian; it is contrary to the opinion that the gallant Captain Courtenay had entertained of him, who had immediately before this given him the charge of a watch in the *Eurydice* throughout the voyage from the East Indies; and it cannot be reconciled with Christian's conduct, which Major Taubman, of the Nunnery in the Isle of Man, can testify, viz that, from his recommendation of Captain Bligh as a navigator, Christian voluntarily preferred sailing with Captain Bligh as a common man in a West India ship, till there was a vacancy among the officers, to the immediate appointment to the rank of a mate in another ship.

Since the publication of the Appendix I have only had an opportunity of seeing two persons belonging to the *Bounty* –

Mr Peckover, the gunner, who lives at No 13 Gun-alley, Wapping; and Mr Purcell, the carpenter, who has since sailed to the West Indies. Mr Purcell declared, in the hearing of James Losh, Esq. of the Temple, that he had read the Appendix, and that every part of it within his knowledge was correctly stated: and Mr Peckover also declared once before John France, Esq. of the Temple, and at another time before John Caley, Esq. of the Augmentation-office that he had read the Appendix, and that every part of it within his knowledge was correctly stated; except that he thought too much praise had been bestowed upon Mr Stewart, though he thought highly of him before the mutiny as a deserving officer. Mr Peckover lives constantly in London, and has the appearance of a cautious, discreet man, and a steady, manly officer; yet no application has been made to him by Captain Bligh respecting the publications.

Lebogue begins his affidavit by stating that I sent for him to a public house; from which the reader would be induced to infer, that I had attempted to seduce these sailors in a corner of a common alehouse falsely to accuse their captain: but as I have already observed, I not only had the precaution to have some gentleman of honour and character in my company, but I also requested several gentlemen to examine the witnesses when I was not present.

Mr Purcell having accidentally mentioned that he was recommended to the *Bounty* by Sir Joseph Banks, and expressing a wish to call upon him, I immediately wrote a note to introduce him to Sir Joseph Banks, and to request Sir Joseph to examine him respecting the causes and circumstances of the mutiny. Having never had an opportunity of seeing Mackintosh (the carpenter's mate) but once, and for a short time, I desired Mr Fearon, a barrister, resident at Newcastle, to inquire for him at Shields, where his mother lived, and to examine him fully upon the subject. Mr Fearon went over to Shields with the Reverend Mr How, of Workington, for that purpose. At the first, Mackintosh was very unwilling to give them any information, saying, that 'he had like to have got into trouble for what he had told Mr Christian in London': but I am authorised to say by these gentlemen, that upon further conversation he confirmed every material circumstance related in the Appendix. Though it may be suspected that I might have an interest or a wish to obtain improper evidence in an improper manner from the witnesses, yet all the gentlemen I have named could only be actuated in their conduct by the purest regard for truth and justice.

Captain Bligh complains that I have not appropriated to each individual the precise and actual information I received from him. If I had requested them to give it in the manner of depositions, they probably would have been deterred from telling anything, as Mackintosh declared he had been threatened for what he had mentioned. I made the first inquiries only for my own satisfaction, as I was assured by another gentleman that he would publish the trial with the information which he had collected; and it was only when he had declined to proceed in it that I was obliged to undertake the painful task myself. But if what I have ventured to communicate to the world in the Appendix is false, it is the grossest libel that ever was published; for which every Judge would be compelled to declare that no punishment could be too severe, or no damages too excessive. Many gentlemen, besides myself, suppose that if any answer could be given, it would be attempted in a court of justice by some judicial proceeding. Indeed the bookseller would not have dared to have sold the Appendix if I had not undertaken to stand between him and danger, and to indemnify him as far as was in my power from the consequences of legal prosecutions. It would scarcely then have been prudent to have disclosed the testimony of each witness, by which I was to defend so hazardous a publication; some of whom, as seafaring men, might easily have been sent into a distant part of the world, and others might perhaps have been induced, like Lebogue, to reverse everything that they had said. But I assert again, and I solemnly appeal to all the gentlemen whose names I have mentioned that in the accounts we received there was no material (if any) contradiction or inconsistency.

The statement in the Appendix has been insidiously called a defence and vindication. God forbid that any connection or consideration should ever induce me to vindicate the crime of mutiny! But though it is a crime which will admit of no defence, yet with respect to its motives and circumstances it is capable of great exaggeration.

I bear no malice to Captain Bligh; and I trust neither love nor fear will ever impel me to shrink from that which I conceive I owe to myself and to society. I solicit no favour I supplicate no mercy. It is to austere and rigorous justice I have made the appeal, which will protect from unmerited obloquy the object of its severest vengeance. Great crimes demand great examples. I will not under any circumstances deprecate, or endeavour to intercept, the stroke of justice. Mine has been a painful duty to discharge; I am happy in knowing that I have discharged it with the approbation of some wise and good men; but I am still happier in feeling that I have discharged it with the approbation of my own heart and conscience.

Edward Christian

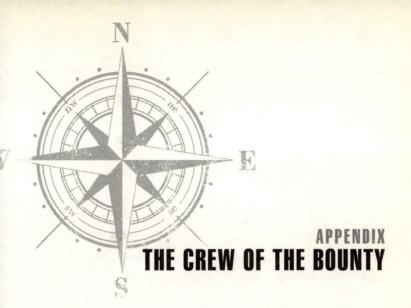

THE CREW OF THE BOUNTY

ADAMS, John
Able Seaman

Used an assumed name: Alexander Smith. Flogged within a week of the *Bounty* first reaching Otaheite, witnessed by locals who were quite distressed by the spectacle. Active participant in the mutiny, and sailed with Christian to Pitcairn. After 1800 the last surviving mutineer on Pitcairn. Pardoned in 1825.

Died Pitcairn, 5th March 1829

BLIGH, William
Commanding Lieutenant

First went to sea aged 7 as captain's personal servant aboard HMS *Monmouth*. Joined the Royal Navy at 15 and was Sailing Master aboard HMS *Resolution* under Captain James Cook at 22. Took command of the *Bounty* 1787. After the mutiny, went on to serve as Governor of New South Wales and ended naval career as Vice Admiral of the Blue.

Died London, 6th December 1817

BROWN, William
Botanist's Assistant

Had served as a Midshipman and Acting Lieutenant previously, but was on the *Bounty* in a civilian capacity. Stayed below decks during mutiny but then chose to stay on board. Went to Pitcairn and was killed in the same massacre as Christian.

Died Pitcairn, 20th September 1793

BURKITT, Thomas
Able Seaman

Helped Christian arrest Bligh during the mutiny. However, he also arranged for Bligh to receive clothes and for the launch to be provided with a compass, despite objections from other mutineers. Chose to stay on Otaheite when Christian continued on to Pitcairn, was arrested when the *Pandora* arrived and survived the sinking. Lacking good counsel at his trial, he was found guilty and sentenced to death.

Hanged aboard HMS *Brunswick*, 29th October 1792

BYRNE, Michael
Able Seaman

Almost blind, he was loyal to Bligh but taken to Otaheite against his will, notionally because his fiddle-playing was popular with the mutineers. Willingly came aboard the *Pandora* and survived the sinking, and was later acquitted of any involvement in the mutiny.

Fate unknown

CHRISTIAN, Fletcher
Master's Mate

Born into landed gentry and went to sea at age 18 as a ship's boy. Originally made Acting Lieutenant in 1784 after only a year's service as Midshipman. Sailed with Bligh on two voyages to the West Indies before the *Bounty* expedition. Bligh made him Second Mate on the second. He also promoted Christian to Acting Lieutenant on the *Bounty* before Christian led the mutiny against him. Died in the massacre on Pitcairn.

Died Pitcairn, 20th September 1793

CHURCHILL, Charles
Master at Arms

Attempted to desert on Otaheite. One of the first to join the mutiny and was Christian's right-hand man throughout. Let off at Otaheite and became chief of Taiarapu until murdered by Matthew Thompson.

Died Otaheite, April 1790

COLE, William
Boatswain

On the receiving end of Bligh's ire on Otaheite after new sails were found to have been affected by mildew, but remained loyal to Bligh, despite Christian discussing desertion with him prior to the mutiny, assuming sympathy if not support. Requested that those being cast adrift be allowed to take the launch and a compass.

Fate unknown

COLEMAN, Joseph
Armourer

A skilled blacksmith and important to the ship, so Christian refused to let him leave even though he was loyal to Bligh. Taken to Otaheite against his will and let off there, and willingly went aboard the *Pandora*, where he was promptly put in irons. Later put on trial but acquitted.

Fate unknown

ELLISON, Thomas
Able Seaman

Joined the *Bounty* aged only 15, having sailed with Bligh on a previous voyage and gaining the captain's favour. When the mutiny began, took up a bayonet and volunteered to stand guard over Bligh. Stayed on Otaheite and gave himself up when the *Pandora* arrived. Survived the sinking and claimed his youth as a defence during the trial. Found guilty and sentenced to death.

Hanged aboard HMS *Brunswick*, 29th October 1792

ELPHINSTON, William
Master's Mate

Asleep when the mutiny began. Remained loyal to Bligh so was cast adrift in the launch, but was not a keen supporter of him during the open-boat voyage. Probably contracted malaria.

Died Batavia, October 1789

FRYER, John
Master

Heavily criticised by Bligh, who gave Christian more authority during the voyage. However, he remained loyal to Bligh, challenging Christian to reconsider the mutiny. He continued to clash with Bligh in the launch, and later helped Edward Christian with his Appendix.

Died Wells-next-the-Sea, Norfolk, 26th May 1817

HALL, Thomas
Cook

Remained loyal to Bligh but probably contracted malaria during the open-boat voyage. During the mutiny he brought provisions up to the launch.

Died Batavia, 11th October 1789

HALLETT, John
Midshipman

Only 15 years old when he joined the *Bounty*. A close friend of Thomas Hayward, and similarly disliked for laziness.

Remained loyal to Bligh but begged to be allowed to stay on board after the mutiny. None of the crew wanted him or Hayward on board, however. He later supported Bligh's version of events.

Died 1794

HAYWARD, Thomas
Midshipman

Close friends with John Hallett, though 12 years his senior. Was part of Christian's watch prior to the mutiny but was asleep on duty. Bligh had put him in irons on Otaheite but gave him commendation after the open-boat journey. A keen supporter of Bligh during the trial of the mutineers. Became Third Lieutenant on the *Pandora*, and survived the sinking, going on to command his own vessel.

Died 1798

HAYWOOD, Peter
Midshipman

Aged 16 at time of the mutiny. Had become good friends with Christian. Played no active part in the mutiny but Bligh believed he had helped plan it. Taken to Otaheite against his will. Willingly went aboard the *Pandora* and was then arrested. Survived the sinking and was later sentenced to death because of Bligh's suspicions. After being pardoned he went on to have a distinguished naval career.

Died 10th February 1831

HILLBRANT, Henry
Able Seaman/Cooper

Born in Hanover and spoke poor English. Was threatened with a flogging by Bligh and was a passive member of the mutiny. Remained on Otaheite after Christian returned there and fled to the mountains when the *Pandora* arrived. Captured and still in irons when the *Pandora* sank.

Died 29th August 1791

HUGGAN, Thomas
Surgeon

His chronic drunkenness led Bligh to try to have him removed from the crew before departure from England. Responsible for the death of James Valentine. Died before the mutiny.

Died Otaheite, 9th December 1788

LAMB, Robert
Butcher

The only man ordered flogged by Bligh who did not later mutiny. Flogged again during the open-boat voyage after eating nine birds caught for food on an island, leaving only twelve to feed everyone else. Contracted a tropical disease in Batavia.

Died at sea en route to Cape Town, 11th October 1789

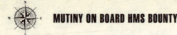

LEBOGUE, Lawrence
Sailmaker

At 40 was one of the oldest amongst the crew. Remained loyal to Bligh but almost died during the open-boat voyage. Later joined Bligh on his second expedition to transport breadfruit.

Fate unknown

LEDWARD, Thomas
Surgeon's Mate

Joined the *Bounty* before she departed England because Bligh knew of Thomas Huggan's chronic drunkenness. Promoted to Surgeon after Huggan's death. Remained loyal to Bligh during the mutiny, but was later highly critical of him. Almost died during the open-boat voyage.

Presumed lost at sea 1789 but reported alive 1791

LINKLETTER, Peter
Quarter-master

Remained loyal to Bligh, but in the launch became openly critical of him after he gave himself extra rations. Imprisoned on a ship in Coupang by Bligh. Believed to have contracted malaria.

Died Batavia, October 1789

MARTIN, Isaac
Able Seaman

Flogged on Otaheite for striking a local who had tried to steal from the *Bounty*'s crew. Was the first man Christian approached with his plan to take over the ship but refused. Later changed his mind, but was not trusted by other mutineers. Joined Christian on journey to Pitcairn and was later killed in the same massacre.

Died Pitcairn, 20th September 1793

M'KOY, William
Able Seaman

One of the first to join the mutiny. Went with Christian to Pitcairn, where he managed to evade being killed in the massacre that claimed Christian and several others. Having worked in a brewery in Glasgow he came up with a way to ferment alcohol and developed an addiction. Whilst drunk he tied a stone around his neck and jumped from a cliff.

Died Pitcairn, 1797

MCINTOSH, Thomas
Carpenter's Crew

Loyal to Bligh but taken to Otaheite against his will because Christian needed his skills as carpenter. Survived the sinking of the *Pandora* and was later tried but acquitted.

Fate unknown

MILLS, John
Gunner's Mate

Helped Christian arrest Bligh during the mutiny, then sailed to Pitcairn with Christian. However, at one point he suggested to several others they abandon Christian. He was killed during the massacre on Pitcairn.

Died Pitcairn, 20th September 1793

MILLWARD, John
Able Seaman

Tried to desert on Otaheite and was flogged. Initially refused to become involved with the mutiny but later took up a musket. Remained on Otaheite and tried to hide in the mountains when the *Pandora* arrived. Caught, survived the sinking, but was later sentenced to death.

Hanged aboard HMS *Brunswick*, 29th October 1792

MORRISON, James
Boatswain's Mate

Nominally loyal to Bligh in that he took no part in the mutiny, but subsequently chose to remain on board the *Bounty*. At trial he claimed he had stayed on board to launch an attempt to retake the ship, but Christian had promoted him after the mutiny, and Morrison was sentenced to death. After being pardoned he continued a naval career, serving as gunner aboard HMS *Blenheim*, which sank in a gale off what is now Reunion Island.

Died 1st February 1807

MUSPRAT, William
Able Seaman/Tailor

Ordered flogged by Bligh on Otaheite, attempted to desert, then received two further floggings. Armed himself with a musket during the mutiny but later claimed he planned to help the officers suppress the uprising. Fled to the mountains when the *Pandora* arrived at Otaheite but was captured, taken back to trial and sentenced to death. Released on appeal, he was later pardoned.

Died aboard HMS *Bellerophon*, 1797

NELSON, David
Botanist

Civilian responsible for selecting breadfruit plants. Had sailed with Bligh and Captain Cook before. Remained loyal to Bligh but almost died during the open-boat voyage. Contracted tropical fever on Timor.

Died Coupang, 20th July 1789

NORMAN, Charles
Carpenter's Mate

Loyal to Bligh but taken to Otaheite against his will because Christian needed his skills as carpenter. Survived the sinking of the *Pandora* and was later tried but acquitted.

Fate unknown

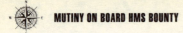

NORTON, John
Quarter-master

Loyal to Bligh, but was killed after the loyalists landed on Tofua and were attacked by locals.

Died Tofua, 3rd May 1789

PECKOVER, William
Gunner

Visited Otaheite several times with Captain James Cook and knew the language so put in charge of trading with locals. Remained loyal to Bligh, even though Bligh later described him as a 'worthless fellow'. Endorsed the version of events in Edward Christian's Appendix.

Fate unknown

PURCELL, William
Carpenter

Had a very antagonistic relationship with Bligh, but still remained loyal during the mutiny. Later assisted Edward Christian with his Appendix. Believed to have been the last survivor of the *Bounty*'s crew when he died.

Died Gosport, 10th March 1834 (reportedly)

QUINTAL, Matthew
Able Seaman

Flogged for 'mutinous behavior' towards John Fryer en route to Cape Horn, though later saved Fryer's life (only two days before mutiny). One of the first Christian approached, and joined the mutiny immediately. Christian himself later put Quintal in irons for disobeying orders. Treated the men and women who joined the ship at Otaheite terribly. Continued to Pitcairn with Christian and set fire to the *Bounty* before the others had removed everything of value and narrowly avoided being killed in the massacre that claimed Christian's life. Killed by John Adams and Ned Young.

Died Pitcairn, 1799

SAMUEL, John
Clerk

Also served as Bligh's personal servant. Was very unpopular with the crew, and mutineers would probably not have allowed him to remain on board, even if he had not remained loyal to Bligh.

Fate unknown

SIMPSON, George
Quarter-master's Mate

Remained loyal to Bligh but was not one of his supporters during the open-boat voyage. Did not give evidence at the trial, which helped the cases of the accused.

Fate unknown

SKINNER, Richard
Able Seaman/Barber

An active participant in the mutiny. Was aiming his musket at someone in the launch (possibly Bligh) when he was inadvertently knocked off aim by another mutineer. Stayed on Otaheite and had a child with a local woman, but was arrested when the *Pandora* arrived and died in irons when she sank.

Died 29th August 1791

SMITH, John
Steward/Cook

Bligh's personal servant. During mutiny was ordered by Christian to serve rum to the mutineers. Testimony at trial helped Peter Haywood and James Morrison. Later joined Bligh on another expedition.

Fate unknown

STEWART, George
Midshipman

Good friends with Christian. Persuaded him not to desert the ship on the raft, but may have inadvertently inspired him to mutiny instead. Mutineers considered him loyal enough to Bligh to put him under guard below decks, and he was taken to Otaheite against his will. Christian made Stewart second in command because he needed him to navigate, but Stewart did not support the mutiny and was unpopular with the men. Was later arrested and taken on board the *Pandora*, still in irons when she sank.

Died 29th August 1791

SUMNER, John
Able Seaman

Last man to be flogged prior to the mutiny, two weeks previously. During mutiny stood guard over John Fryer and kept other loyalists from coming up on deck. Christian later put Sumner in arms for disobedience. Chose to stay on Otaheite when the *Bounty* left and tried to hide in the mountains when the *Pandora* arrived. Captured and still in irons when the *Pandora* sank.

Died 29th August 1791

THOMPSON, Matthew
Able Seaman

Widely considered most brutal member of the *Bounty*'s crew, and popular with none. Flogged on Otaheite. One of the first to join the mutiny, standing guard over the arms chest to prevent those loyal to Bligh arming themselves. Remained on Otaheite when the *Bounty* left and later murdered Charles Churchill and several locals. He was killed in retaliation.

Died Otaheite, April 1790

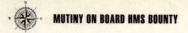

TINKLER, Robert
Midshipman

John Fryer's brother-in-law. Loyal to Bligh, but was not one of his supporters during the open-boat voyage. Later promoted to Commander after the Battle of Copenhagen, 1801.

Fate unknown

VALENTINE, James
Able Seaman

The first of the crew to die, several weeks before the *Bounty* first reached Otaheite. Surgeon Thomas Huggan treated what may have been an asthma attack by bleeding him. Valentine's wound became gangrenous and the infection killed him.

Died 9th October 1788

WILLIAMS, John
Able Seaman/Armourer's Mate

Having been ordered flogged by Bligh, Williams took an active part in the mutiny and went with Christian to Pitcairn. An argument over a woman led to the massacre that killed him, Christian and others.

Died Pitcairn, 20th September 1793

YOUNG, Edward
Midshipman

The only officer to join Christian, but took no active part in the mutiny himself. Some have conjectured that he may have helped Christian plan it. Also some evidence he was behind massacre on Pitcairn that killed Christian and several other mutineers.

Died Pitcairn, 25th December 1800